The SAILOR and The "Miracle Ship":

B. P. Edwards CZM

Benjamin P. (Pete) Edwards,
Crew Member
and
Olan Bassham

To: RAY
*With Every Good Wish
And The Best Of Health*

TO BUY POSTAGE FREE
Send Check or Money Order For $18.00 To:

B. P. EDWARDS
76 Rolling Meadows
Goodlettsville, TN 37072

I MAIL TO ANY PLACE IN THE U.S.A.

The Sailor & The Miracle Ship

Capt. C. H. Roper of the U.S.S. New Orleans

The SAILOR and The "Miracle Ship":
The Saga of the U.S.S. New Orleans in World War II

Benjamin P. (Pete) Edwards,
Crew Member
and
Olan Bassham

Heritage Press
4035 Emerald Drive
Murfreesboro, TN 37130

Copyright © 1999 Benjamin P. Edwards. All rights reserved. No part of this material may be reproduced in any form without written permission from the publisher, except for brief quotes in reviews.

First printing 1999.

Library of Congress Cataloging-in-Publication Data
_____

Edwards, Benjamin P., Author
Bassham, Olin, Author
"The Sailor and The 'Miracle' Ship: The Saga of the U.S.S. New Orleans in WWII"
ISBN 1-889332-26-7

Cover: The Author as a seventeen year old crew member of the U.S.S. New Orleans.

Background: The New Orleans with 120 feet blown off after a Japanese attack.

DEDICATION

To Shipmates, Family and Friends
and particularly to

Vice Admiral P.N. Charbonnet
Capt. Clifford H. Roper
Chaplain H. Forgey*
Master Chief John R. Burton, Jr.
Mr. Olan Bassham

* Chaplain Forgey of The USS New Orleans was credited with the phrase "Praise The Lord and Pass The Ammunition" during the Japanese attack on Pearl Harbor Dec. 7, 1941. This rallying cry was later the basis for a famous WWII song of the same name.

The Sailor & The Miracle Ship

Master Chief Boatswain's Mate John R. Burton, Jr.

The Sailor & The Miracle Ship

Vice Admiral P. N. Charbonnet, one time Lt. (JG) aboard
The U.S.S. New Orleans in WW II.

Table of Contents

Preface……………………………………………………….iv
Introduction………………………………………………..viii
Prologue……………………………………………………..ix
Dedication…………………………………………………..xv
Chapter 1……………………………………………………..1
Chapter 2……………………………………………………13
Chapter 3……………………………………………………19
Chapter 4……………………………………………………23
Chapter 5……………………………………………………29
Chapter 6……………………………………………………35
Chapter 7……………………………………………………39
Chapter 8……………………………………………………51
Chapter 9……………………………………………………57
Chapter 10…………………………………………………..67
Chapter 11…………………………………………………..79

Table of Contents (continued)

Chapter 12..85

Chapter 13..87

Chapter 14..95

Chapter 15..103

Chapter 16..109

Chapter 17..119

Chapter 18..121

Chapter 19..139

Chapter 20..147

Epilogue..155

Speech..161

Preface

Benjamin Porter Edwards, Jr. saw a movie when he was ten years of age that kindled in him the burning desire to become a "Navy man." At the age of sixteen when he heard about the sneak attack of Japan on Pearl Harbor, his anger added fuel to that desire to the point that he lied about his age and joined the Navy. Within a few months this boy was flung into one of the fiercest and most destructive Naval battles of World War II. It was the battle of Tassafornga in the Solomons to hold Guadalcanal for the Americans. It was vital to winning the war against Japan. If Japan could control Guadalcanal and the Solomon Islands it would be a jumping off place for them to control the South Pacific in their expansion toward the Hawaiian Islands with eyes fixed on the U. S. mainland. When you read this book you'll see how a boy sailor who's mother had to sign for him to get into the Navy became an "Old Salt" overnight and then went on to be the recipient of five gold stars to wear on his campaign ribbon for participation in five major battles.

The fiercest and perhaps the most important battle young Edwards was in was the battle to save Guadalcanal in which his ship the U.S.S. Heavy Cruiser, the New

Orleans was involved. As a result of the damage inflicted on the New Orleans and the efforts to save her to fight again, she has been dubbed the "Miracle Ship." Although Task Force 67 ships suffered severe damage, they saved Guadalcanal and at the same time it was a tremendous morale builder for the Americans and at the same time a devastating blow to the morale of Japan. In this regard, the battle of Tassafaronga to save Guadalcanal could well have been a turning point of the war with Japan.

Olan Bassham

Introduction

I truly hope these details of how the U.S.S. New Orleans survived the battle of Tassaronga near Guadalcanal in the Pacific area of World War II, will help you to see that the gallant ship was every inch what she has been dubbed, "The Miracle Ship" that saved itself and refused to sink.

After you read this book, I'm sure some of you will be wondering how after 56 years I can relate with pinpoint accuracy all these events. The secret is, I kept a diary while I was in the Navy. It was bitterly against the rules, but I couldn't resist. I wrote my diary in outline form and put it in my clothes in my locker. Each time I came home on leave, I'd write it out in detail and leave the completed part of the diary.

One day I was telling my minister, Olan Bassham, about the battle of Tassaronga and he was so impressed that he asked me to write a book about my Naval experiences. He said that if I would he would help me write and edit it and help me get it published. I thought, "What have I got to lose?" While the title of the book is "The Sailor & The Miracle Ship" and details relating to that terrible Naval battle at Guadalcanal, other interesting facts of my Navy life are included. Also included are facts of my early life leading right on up to my joining the Navy at the tender age of sixteen.

We send this book out with the hope and prayer that it will accomplish the greatest possible good.

B. P. Edwards

Prologue

On August 8, 1942, the American Public read in their morning paper that United States Marines had landed on Guadalcanal and Talagi Islands in the South Pacific. To that time very few people had ever heard of those islands or the Solomon group of islands where there was such fierce fighting on part of our Navy, Marines, Airforce and Army. For the next year hardly a day passed but what Guadalcanal was in the news.

The mountainous islands of the Solomons group was only 90 miles long by 25 miles wide. It was inhabited by a few wooly-haired Melanesians, mud, coconuts, and malarial mosquitoes. It was bitterly contested by Naval, Air, and Ground forces of the United States and Japan for almost six months. There were six major Naval engagements within a period of only four months. They were very costly both in men and in ships. You will search the seven seas in vain for an ocean graveyard with the bones of so many ships and sailors as that body of water between Guadalcanal, Savo, and Florida Islands which our Blue Jackets named "Iron Bottom Sound."

Six weeks before the operation began, the United States knew little more of the Solomon Islands than did the public. The union officers and Blue Jackets knew more about the moon than they knew about Guadalcanal and the Solomon Islands. The Islands had never figured in the prewar plans of the United States Navy. The Marines usually prepared to land anywhere at any time. They had information on almost every group of Pacific Islands, except the Solomons. A hasty search for more data in Australia yielded little. Some of them described Guadalcanal as a "bloody, stinking hole" which is what it was. Situated right under the line between latitudes 5 degrees and 11 degrees south, the Solomons are wet, hot, and steamy. There is no difference between seasons except more rainfalls between November and March. The islands are jagged, lofty and volcanic on Guadalcanal, the mountains rising to 8000 feet above the sea.

For almost two centuries the Solomon Islands were forgotten. Royal hydrographers assumed that they had never existed. If that had been true, the United States Navy, Army, Airforce and Marines would have been well pleased and well served. Around 1767 Guadalcanal was rediscovered by a great French Navigator, The Sier De Bougainville for whom the big northern island is named. Lieutenant Shortland followed in 1778 and named a small island after himself and big one after his king, New Georgia.

By that time, nobody wanted the Solomons. There was not enough gold to attract prospectors, and the islands were too remote, sinister and devoid of game to impress pleasure seekers. "Blackbirders" looking for slave labor to use in Queensland, Australia on sugar plantations would pull raids now and then.

During the last two decades of the nineteenth century, when European powers divided up the Pacific Islands, Germany annexed Bougainville, while Great Britain took the rest of the Solomons. The Australian Airforce stationed a squadron of Catalinas in Gavury Harbor near Tulugi and assigned twenty infantrymen to help the "Gilbert and Sullivan Army" of 15 whites and 5 Chinese and 130 native police in defending their base. Japanese planes began making bombing runs on Tulagi and Gavury in January, 1942. The European and Chinese shopkeepers started getting out. When the Jap Task Force, part of the Coral Sea operation, approached on May 1st, the Australian government saw that defense was hopeless and ordered Talagi to be evacuated.

The Japanese "Promised the Islanders the moon," but they were very tough on those who didn't toe the mark. Their maltreatment of the natives made them eager to have the white men back.

The one thing that outlasted the Japanese invasion was the Australian "Coast Watchers." They were a network of small radio stations throughout the Solomons, established several years earlier and taken over by the Australian Navy in 1939. Their reports of enemy movements was invaluable at a time when American airpower was worn thin and the Japs had an advantage all over the Pacific. It was generally felt that if Japan could gain and hold complete control; the Solomon Islands would become a springboard for attacks on Australia and New Zealand. I know of no other outfit in the world like the Australian "Coast Watchers." Only eight or nine of them remained in the Solomons after the evacuation of Tulagi. Many others were brought back by American boats or planes. These "Coast Watchers" whom the natives generally aided, played a valuable part in American successes in that part of the South Pacific. They relayed to Allied Headquarters the movements of enemy ships, planes and ground forces. Their reports of southward flying enemy aircraft, received as much as fifty minutes in advance, made it possible for American planes to take off and gain altitude in time to swoop down on the enemy and blow them out of the sky. So, we hereby salute the "Coast Watchers" in particular and our unforgettable Allied country "Down Under" in general. With United States forces engaged in warfare some 7,000 miles away from our shores, Australia quickly became our home away from home.

I have not forgotten the way the "Aussies" rolled out the red carpet to the U.S.S. New Orleans and her crew on Christmas Eve, 1942 when we arrived in Sydney. It seemed as though they couldn't do enough for us. Without the repair work they did on our ship, we could have never made it back to the United States.

B. P. Edwards, Jr. (Pete) BMC, retired

Dedication

We proudly dedicate this book to Master Chief Boatswain Mate John R. Burton, Jr., who after his active tour of Navy duty, distinguished himself by his leadership role in the Naval Reserve of Nashville, Tennessee. He was so dedicated to making the Nashville Center the best possible that the word got out that they had more Chiefs than White Hats in that center. It was said that "Chief Burton looks after his men like a mother hen looks after her baby chicks." His study methods and counseling was commended at the 6th and 8th Districts. Under Chief Burton's guidance and training, the Nashville Center became a model that other Naval Reserve Centers over the nation copied.

We don't feel that the dedication of this book should be limited to one person. So we share the dedication to Navy Commanders such as Captain Clifford H. Roper and Rear Admiral Pierre Charbonnet who were both on the "Miracle Ship" New Orleans in the battle of Tassafornga when almost one fourth of the ship was blown away by three power blasts. The first by Japanese torpedo, setting off the two magazines of the ship, in turn, triggering the third blast of the seven thousand gallon fuel reserve.

Captain Roper was the brilliant Commander of the New Orleans and through his wise leadership "the most damaged ship ever, not to sink" was saved to fight the enemy again. Pierre Charbonnet was seaman Pete Edward's (subject of this book) Junior Division Officer during this strategic and even decisive battle to save Guadalcanal. Pierre Charbonnet went on to rise to the rank of Rear Admiral in charge of the entire U. S. Naval Reserve.

We would surely be remiss if we did not include in this dedication the hundreds of brave men who served on the New Orleans that awful night of battle in Lengo Channel to prevent Japan from landing troops on Guadalcanal. One hundred and seventy-eight sailors lost their lives on the ship that night and 23 were wounded. Dedication, with deep appreciation, goes to the others in Task Force 67 who fought so bravely, many of them giving their lives, on that night of November 30, 1942, in the steamy Solomon Islands.

To these and every one who served to preserve the precious freedom America enjoys, we are eternally grateful.

❧ 1 ❧

He was trembling as he stepped on the deck of the U.S.S. New Orleans, long since mothballed. Memories flooded his mind of that terrible night of November 30, 1942 near Guadalcanal when a Japanese naval unit demolished the American naval task force of which he was a part. He first walked slowly over the bow of this gallant heavy cruiser. This bow had replaced the original one that had been blown totally off by torpedo the night of the battle. He then made his way down into his battlestation which was the powder room of Turret 3 where he was a Powder Handler. As he reminisced he could still feel that awful thud and the jolt that ripped off almost one fourth of the length of the New Orleans. Chief Petty Officer Benjamin Edwards knew full well why this magnificent ship had been dubbed the Miracle Ship because he was a part of it all.

The Sailor & The Miracle Ship

As he sat there and wept he let his mind drift back to his early beginnings and even to what his mother had told him about his birth: The doctor holds the newborn by his feet bottom side up and slaps him on the rump. The baby lets out a loud cry. He weighs in at 10 ½ pounds.

"Mrs. Edwards," the doctor said, "You've got a fine, healthy boy and he's a big 'un. He'll likely make a good guard in football. From the size of him it won't be long 'till he makes the team."

"Just so he's healthy, doctor," Mrs. Edwards said. "That's what matters most and this day I dedicate him to his God and his country."

"That's a most noble ambition for the boy, Mrs. Edwards," the doctor said. "Have you picked out a name for him?"

The Sailor & The Miracle Ship

Mrs. Edwards looks up to her husband who is standing by the bed. "Benjamin, since he's our first born, let's name him for you and make him a junior."

"That'll be fine Martha. I'm honored. Benjamin Porter, Jr.. That's got a good ring to it. Let's call him Pete for short."

"Mr. and Mrs. Edwards, I don't foresee any problems for the baby," the doctor said. "But keep a close watch on him and call me if you need me."

"Thanks, Doctor," Mr. Edwards said. "We'll do that."

A month later Mrs. Edwards could tell that little Pete was not growing. If anything he seemed to be losing ground. She called the doctor and explained the situation. The doctor didn't seem to be concerned, just recommended another formula for the baby. After two months of the

The Sailor & The Miracle Ship

new formula, little Pete still seemed to be losing ground. Mrs. Edwards spoke to her husband about her concerns:

"Benjamin, this baby is not doing any good. There must be something seriously wrong with him."

"I know Martha. He looks like he is losing weight daily. If something is not done for him, we could lose him. What's that doctor's name that delivered him?"

"Dr. Joseph Ardmore."

"Get an appointment with him as soon as possible and we'll take little Pete to his office."

On the appointment day, Dr. Ardmore examined little Pete carefully and didn't find the cause of weight loss.

"It's not unusual for a baby to lose some weight in the first week or so," Dr. Ardmore said. "But little Pete's case is unusual. I'm recommending a special enriched formula. Try him on that for a while. I think that'll bring him out of it."

The Sailor & The Miracle Ship

After a few weeks of the enriched formula, little Pete was still losing weight. After six months on different formulas where nothing worked, a pediatrician found that his esophagus at the passageway to his stomach was practically closed allowing a bare trickle of milk or formula to his stomach. While at birth little Pete weighed 10 ½ pounds, at the end of six months he weighed six pounds.

"Mr. and Mrs. Edwards," the doctor said. "Your baby needs to be breast fed. I suggest you find some new mothers in your area and see if some of them will help breast feed him."

They found some new mothers willing to cooperate and the problem corrected itself. That little six pound sick boy grew to be a 250 pound man.

One of Pete Edward's first recollections was a photographer who came through his neighborhood riding a cart pulled by goats. Pete's mother had his picture taken

The Sailor & The Miracle Ship

on the cart but that wasn't enough for Pete, he wanted the cart and the goats.

When Pete was fifteen months of age a baby girl was born to Mr. and Mrs. Benjamin Edwards. In their childhood Pete and his sister were inseparable. They were so close that people called them Pete and Re-Pete. If anyone hurt or threatened to harm "Sis" they would have to answer to Pete.

Years move swiftly by to Pete's 12th birthday. He found a good secondhand bicycle that he talked his parents into buying for him. The brand name was Rollfast. Pete loved that bicycle so much that he slept with it in his bedroom.

One day Pete was playing ball in East Part when a friend named Bill Banks approached him.

"Pete, I've got you a job."

The Sailor & The Miracle Ship

"But I don't want a job. I'd rather play."

"Aw, Pete, I've already asked Doc Cook to give you a job. At least go talk to him."

"All right, but what kind of job is it?"

"Delivering prescription orders on your bike. That's made to order for you. Go check it out."

"Okay, I will when I finish this game."

That afternoon Pete rode his bicycle to the Mose Cook Drug Store on Seventh Street. He walked past the soda fountain and looked longingly at the banana-split the soda-jerk was making for a customer. He made his way back to the prescription counter where Doc Cook was mixing a prescription."

"How you doing Pete? I'll be with you in a minute."

The Sailor & The Miracle Ship

Doc Cook finished his prescription and walked around to where Pete was standing and looked down at him over his horn-rim glasses.

"Pete, what's this I hear about you wanting a job?"

"Aw, I don't know, Doc," not knowing what to say because he, like every twelve year old boy, had rather play than work.

"They tell me Pete, that you like to ride a bicycle and I can use you to deliver prescriptions. Do you want the job?"

"I'll think about it Doc," Pete said as he turned to walk away.

"Wait a minute, son. I'm not through talking. If you work for me, I don't mind if you get a candy bar and an ice cream cone now and then. I don't pay that any attention."

The Sailor & The Miracle Ship

This appealed to Pete.

"What does the job pay, Doc?"

"Three dollars a week, Pete."

"The money sounds good," Pete said. "I'll take it."

"You'll need a social security card."

"What's that?"

"It's a new law that requires us to withhold from your wages a certain amount which goes to the government."

"Where do I get that card?"

"Go over to the Cotton States Building. They'll give you one."

Pete rode his bike across the Woodland Street Bridge on Cumberland River. He walked barefooted into the Social Security office and up to the desk of the receptionist.

The Sailor & The Miracle Ship

"What do you need?" the receptionist said with a smile.

"I need a Social Security card," Pete said, stuttering as he tried to pronounce the term.

"Why do you need a Social Security card?" she said with a giggle, looking down at his bare feet.

"I'm gonna work for the Mose Cook Drug Store and Doc Cook said I'd have to have one."

Those who processed Pete's card were both amused and amazed at this twelve year old, barefooted boy and his Social Security card. Young Edwards is introduced to the world of economics and on his way to greater heights.

One day when Pete was delivering prescriptions a dog attacked him from behind and ripped out the seat of his pants. In his embarrassment he found a posterboard and held it behind him as he knocked on the door of a black lady to deliver her prescription.

The Sailor & The Miracle Ship

"Son, what are you doing with that posterboard behind you?" the lady asked.

"A dog tore the seat of my pants out."

"Come on in this house boy an I'll fix your pants."

Pete never forgot that kind lady sewing up his pants.

The Sailor & The Miracle Ship

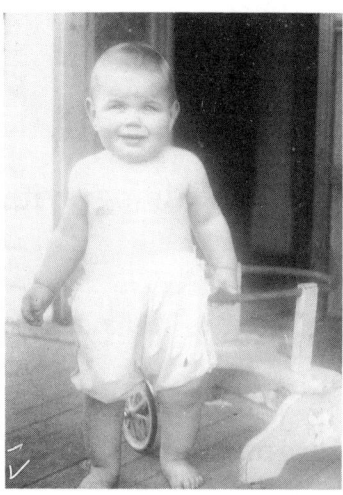

Young Pete Edwards (age 2 ?)

≈ 2 ≈

When Pete was thirteen, there was something that changed his life and his ambition for life. He saw a movie based on navy life, called *"Don't Give Up The Ship,"* starring Dick Powell. From that day on his greatest desire was to join the navy and that time was not far off.

When Pete was sixteen, on Sunday morning December 7, 1941, he was playing football in East Park of his hometown Nashville, Tennessee. Sis rode down to the park on Pete's bicycle. When he looked up and saw her riding his bicycle, he knew something was wrong because he forbade Sis to ride his bicycle. He saw she was upset and excited.

"What's wrong Sis?"

"Oh, Pete, the Japs have bombed Pearl Harbor."

"What's Pearl Harbor, where's that?"

The Sailor & The Miracle Ship

"I don't know, but it's all over the radio."

Pete doubled his sister back home on the bicycle. He hit the door begging his mother to let him join the navy.

"Mama, I wanna join the navy, will you sign for me?"

"I certainly will not!"

"Why not, Mama? I wanna go real bad."

"'Cause you're just a child, and what's more I need you at home to help out. Besides, we need the money the drugstore pays you for delivering prescription orders on your bicycle."

"But Mama, the navy pay will be more than that and I'll send it back home every month."

"It's settled, Pete. You might as well shut up. And another thing, what makes you think the navy will accept you at your age?"

The Sailor & The Miracle Ship

"Mama, I'm big for my age. I'll fib about my age. They'll accept me if you'll just sign for me."

"Case closed, forget it. Go on back to the park and play."

Pete knew his mother meant business. When she felt she was right about a matter, it was hard to change her mind. But he wasn't about to give up. To be a navy man was his great dream.

All through that winter, spring and summer, Pete continued to pester his mother to let him join the navy. He knew just how far to go in pressing the matter. But he was persistent because he was not about to give up on the fulfillment of that most cherished dream.

With his size and weight Pete was a good candidate for football, but he couldn't keep his mind on football, school, or anything else but the navy.

The Sailor & The Miracle Ship

Pete said to himself, "I'll finish this school year and before school starts again I'll be in the navy." He had been exposed to some of Norman Vincent Peal's book, "The Power Of Positive Thinking". He thought, "If I think and act like a navy man, I will be a navy man."

He went down to the Military Surplus store and fitted himself with a navy uniform. He thought, "I'll put on this uniform and walk in and surprise Mama and make her think I lied about my age and joined the navy. Maybe, just maybe, that'll convince her and she'll sign for me and let me join."

He walked into the house back to the kitchen where his mother was preparing supper. "Look, Mama, I'm in the navy at last."

When Mrs. Edwards turned and saw him, she almost fainted.

The Sailor & The Miracle Ship

When he saw how disturbed she was, Pete hugged her.

"Naw, Mama, I'm just kidding. I bought this uniform at the surplus store. I thought this would help persuade you to sign for me."

"Well, son, if you feel that strong about it I won't hold you back, I hate to do it, but I'll sign for you."

A surge of joy filled Pete's very being as he let out a shout of joy, "Thank you Mama, thank you. You won't regret it. I'll make you proud of me."

"I hope I won't regret it, son. These are troubled and dangerous times, what with the whole world at war. And son, I want you to know I'm already proud of you, navy or no navy. We'll miss you son. I'll be praying for your safe return."

The Sailor & The Miracle Ship

"I know you will, Mama. You and Sis will be okay. This is a good neighborhood, good friends and neighbors here on Russell Street. You'll make it fine."

3

It is late in the summer of 1942, August 14. Pete Edwards had slept very little last night, excited about joining the navy. His Mother had arisen at 6:00 a.m. to prepare breakfast and to help Pete pack. Pete and Sis got up about 6:30 and they're seated around the table having breakfast.

"Pete, enjoy your breakfast. Eat hearty son for this is the last meal you'll have at home for a while."

Pete could see a tear on her cheek. He glanced at Sis and saw tears in her eyes.

"Hey, you girls stop that crying. Be happy for me. This is my life's dream. This is what I was born for."

"I know Pete," Sis replied. "But you and I have been so close. Remember Dad dubbed us Pete and Re-Pete. I'll be lost without you."

"Oh, you'll be okay Sis. You'll make friends with girls near your age and stop being so much a tomboy."

The Sailor & The Miracle Ship

Pete then turns to his mother. "Mama, I'll ride my bicycle across the river to the Federal Building. You and Sis drive over so you can sign for me to enlist and Sis can ride my bicycle back home. Take good care of my bicycle. It's meant a lot to me. It's been a trusty friend."

"Don't worry about your bike son. We'll take good care of it."

"Thanks, Mama. Now I've got to do some packing and take care of some odds and ends. I have to be at the Federal Building by 2:00."

"Okay son. Your Aunt Katherine will drive us over there. You can ride your bike behind us."

The Navy Petty Officer that did the swearing in announced that any man who had changed his mind about going into the navy could fall out, and nothing would be said; but once sworn in it would be too late.

The Sailor & The Miracle Ship

"Son, fall out," Pete's mother pled. "You're under age. Don't let yourself be sworn in."

"Mama, this is what I want to do. You've known for years my ambition has been to join the Navy. It'll be okay."

Kathrine Lewis, Pete's Aunt, was in ill health at an early age by working hard and long hours. When Pete raised his right hand and was sworn in, his Aunt fainted and his mother screamed.

The Sailor & The Miracle Ship

Seaman Edwards (1942)

4

On his 17th birthday, September 1, 1942, Pete Edwards is doing boot camp in San Diego, California. On the long train ride from Nashville to San Diego, he had felt a tinge of homesickness. After all he had been a home boy, seldom spending a night away from home. But any homesickness was soon to end in boot camp. No time to think much about home during the hard training and too tired and sleepy to be homesick at night.

At boot camp the rule was that every day when the trainees came in from marching they had to wash their clothes out on the patio. One afternoon Pete did not finish his. He wanted to see a good movie and this would be his last chance to see it. He had planned to finish his laundry when he returned, but he forgot. The next morning Chief Boatswain Mate Westfall approached Pete:

"Edwards, is that your bucket of clothes?"

The Sailor & The Miracle Ship

"Yes Sir," Pete replied in a loud clear voice.

"Go to the barracks and bring me the short line from your hammock."

When Pete brought the short line, the Chief tied it to the bucket, then tied the bucket around Pete's neck and made him wear that bucket of clothes all day. Pete never forgot to do his laundry again.

Upon completing boot camp, they sailed the Pacific toward the Solomon Islands for action against the Japanese who were taking the Islands at will. Pete committed himself to learning as much about that heavy cruiser New Orleans as he possibly could. He asked questions of superiors, he took notes, he sketched drawings of the works of the ship. He learned that the main battery was 8 inch guns, with three gun Turrets, which fired 8 inch diameter projectiles. The air defense consisted of 20 and 40 millimeter guns. Numbering of the gun Turrets starts at

The Sailor & The Miracle Ship

the forward part of the ship and increases as you go aft. Edwards was assigned to the 3rd Division. His battle station was in the lower Powder Handling room of Turret 3, at the bottom of the Turret and below the water line. Through intensive drills and training every man knew exactly what to do in time of action. They also knew the duties of other battle stations around so they could take over from a fallen gun crew member on short notice. During his time on the New Orleans, there was only one battle station in a Turret that young Edwards did not man and that was gun captain.

His division officer offered that station to him but he declined feeling that was too much responsibility due to his young age. You have to remember, most of Edwards time in the navy was time spent as a teenager.

His favorite station in the Turret was that of a Ramer in the gun room of the Turret. He rams the

The Sailor & The Miracle Ship

projectile into the gun. There is more action in the gun room than any other place on the Turret because there are more men in that station. Edwards learned so much about the Turrets that he could name the positions and their activities; The Trainer moves the guns around horizontally. The Pointer elevates and lowers the gun. There is a Gun Captain for each of the three guns. After the guns have been fired each Gun Captain working in unison sets off a blast of compressed air inside the guns which blows out the gas and prevents it from coming in the gun room when the breach of the guns are opened. For each of the three guns there is a Ramerman and a Powder Handler. Then there is the Division Officer who is in charge of the Turret.

An 8 inch armor piercing projectile weights 260 pounds and two 55 pound bags of powder are required to fire it. Young Edwards even learned the different colors of the various projectiles: Target practice, maroon; Anti-aircraft or bombardment, green; Star shells, blue; Armor projectile, black. He learned that the powder bags were made of silk because silk burns very quickly and leaves hardly any residue. One end of the powder bag is red, meaning the explosive charge is in that end. Edwards further learned that a Turret gun can be fired by the Pointer, Trainer or by the Division Officer. It could also be fired from the Bridge. Edwards stored all these facts in his mind so he could perform a variety of services if called upon.

The Sailor & The Miracle Ship

Seaman Edwards and Shipmates

❧ 5 ❧

The U.S.S. New Orleans arrived at Pearl Harbor October 4, 1942. On the way over, Pete had met and struck up a friendship with a sailor from Spokane Washington named M. L. Coyle. Coyle was the kind that was mild-mannered until he got a few beers under his belt, and then he got rambunctious and wanted to have his way right or wrong. As they approached Pearl Harbor, although it had been eight months since the bombing, the yard workers were still repairing the damaged ships.

"Them dirty lowdown Japs," Coyle said. "I can't wait to kick their lousy butts."

"It looks like you'll get that chance soon," Pete said. "We're leaving Pearl in a week or two and heading right into the thick of things."

"Edwards, did you get seasick on the way here?"

The Sailor & The Miracle Ship

"Yeah M. L., I puked a couple of times, but then I got over it.:

"You pollywog, you ought to be tough like me. Seasickness don't bother me."

"We'll see about that. You may not be out of the woods yet. Mama always told me, 'Don't count your chickens before they hatch.'"

"Say, Edwards, we get shore leave tomorrow. Let's go into Honolulu, see some sights and get a tattoo. A sailor needs a tattoo, you know."

"I'll go with you to Honolulu but I don't want a tattoo."

"Yeah, you're gonna get a tattoo. Josh Hemrick another friend of mine is going with us and we'll all three get a tattoo."

"I told you M. L. and that's final. I'm not gonna get a tattoo."

The Sailor & The Miracle Ship

Coyle saw that Edwards meant business so he dropped the subject for the time being. However, the subject of tattoos was soon to cause trouble between Coyle and Edwards.

The next day Edwards, Coyle and Hemrick headed out on their liberty into Honolulu. Edwards and Hemrick were wearing gas masks strapped to their shoulders while Coyle didn't have one.

"M. L., Where's your gas mask?" Edwards asked. "That's orders. After what the Japs have done to Pearl Harbor, who knows but what they will sneak some planes in and drop poisonous gas on the city."

"I ain't gonna wag no gas mask around," Coyle said.

"Have it your way," Edwards said. "But if we meet a M.P. you're in trouble."

The Sailor & The Miracle Ship

When they arrived in town they found a tattoo shop. They walked in and Coyle explained the type of tattoo he wanted. Pete waited patiently and when the tattoo artist was finished with Coyle, it was Hemrick's turn.

"Take a look Edwards," Coyle said as he proudly stretched out his arm for Pete to see. The tattoo consisted of a heart with a dagger through it and the words, C. M. Coyle, Spokane, Washington.

As Pete took a look he never dreamed what a source of sadness and distress that tattoo would be to him less than two months later.

Hemrick finished his tattoo and they headed out to see the town. Coyle spotted a tavern and suggested they get a few beers.

"I don't drink," Edwards said. "My Mama showed me in the Bible that strong drink is a mocker and it bites like a serpent."

The Sailor & The Miracle Ship

"Mama's baby," Coyle said with sarcasm and Hemrick laughed.

While Pete felt a little anger, he let it pass.

"I'll go in with you boys and drink a coke," Pete said.

As Coyle is finishing his fourth beer he turns and speaks to Josh Hemrick.

"We got our tattoos but Sissy here didn't get one," as he points to Pete.

"Let's make him get one Hemrick."

Hemrick agrees and they each get Edwards by an arm and proceed to drag him out.

"Boys, I'm not getting a tattoo, turn me loose."

They pay Edwards no attention but keep pulling him toward the door.

Edwards shakes himself free and reaches from the floor with an uppercut to Coyle's chin and sends him

The Sailor & The Miracle Ship

crashing over a table, flat on his back and out like a light. Hemrick turns and runs but Pete hits him with a flying tackle. While Pete is roughing up Hemrick, two M.P.'s walk in the door and pull Pete off.

"Hey Sailors," one M.P. said, "Don't waste that energy whipping up on one another. Save it to whip the Japs. What's your station?"

"We're on the U.S.S. New Orleans in the harbor," Pete said.

"Well, we'll let you go this time but you'd best take your buddies back to the ship."

"Yes Sir," Pete said, glad to get off so lightly.

Coyle was reviving and Hemrick was roughed up slightly but neither of them any worse for the wear. They walked back together to the ship and Pete had no more hassle with his buddies.

6

The New Orleans crossed the equator on November 16, 1942 heading for action in the Solomon Islands.

"Well, we just crossed the Equator," Pete said to Coyle.

"What's the equator? I didn't see nothing."

Pete grinned. "It's nothing you can see, Coyle. It's an imaginary circle around the earth equal distance at all points from the North Pole and the South Pole. And there's something else I've heard and we'd better be ready for it."

"What's that," Coyle said with a concerned look on his face.

"I hear when the ship crosses the equator, that's when Pollywogs Apprentice Seamen get initiated by the Shellbacks."

The Sailor & The Miracle Ship

At that moment the announcement came over the public address, "All Apprentice Seamen report to upper deck promptly."

When they were assembled on deck a Seaman First Class spoke in a stern voice, "Men we have a few things we want you lowly no good pollywogs to do. See that garbage shute over there," as he points to the shute. I want you men to line up in single file and each one of you, one by one, crawl through that shute. There'll be one of us Shellbacks there to direct you in. You'll be greeted by another Shellback on the other end. You'll each get a nice bath, a good haircut, a fine supper and then you should be ready for a good night's sleep."

As each man bent over to enter the garbage shute, he received a shark whack on the rump with a paddle. As he made his way through the garbage out the other end he was greeted by the strong force of a fire hose which

The Sailor & The Miracle Ship

knocked him to the deck and hosed him clean. When the last man was through the shute, they were all given dry clothes and ordered to the ship's barber shop. One by one they were asked by the barber, "How do you want your hair cut?" and one by one they received a shaved head. They were assembled in the ship's mess hall where there was waiting for them some of the navy's best chow. They were deprived of silverware and were forced to eat their food with their hands while the Shellbacks looked delightfully on.

Edwards thought, "The one good thing about this initiation, I'm no longer a lowly Pollywog, I've been converted to a trusty Shellback."

The Sailor & The Miracle Ship

Seaman Edwards at the wheel of an L.C.V.P.
(Landing Craft Vehicle Personnel)

7

Enroute to the Solomon Islands Captain Clifford H. Roper, commander of the New Orleans, called a meeting of the ship's personnel to make an important announcement":

"Men, we received our orders. We're to be a part of Task Force 67. We've been ordered to rendezvous on November 28 with the rest of our ships at Guadalcanal for further instructions. The task force will be under the general command of Rear Admiral Carleton H. Wright. Task Force 67 will consist of four heavy cruisers, including our own; one light cruiser and six destroyers. Gentlemen, that's some task force. You can be proud to be a part of it. All I ask is that you do your best and you'll do your country proud. That's all men. Do what you've been trained to do and do it well."

On November 28, the New Orleans met the rest of the task force and received further instructions. An enemy

The Sailor & The Miracle Ship

force of seven destroyers and six transports was expected off Guadalcanal on the night of November 30 to land Japanese troops on the island in an attempt to drive American Marines off. It was vitally important that the island be held because it contained the only American airfield in that area. Earlier on that day a dispatch was issued by Admiral Halsey for Task Force 67 to intercept the Japanese force.

Japanese Rear Admiral Raizo Tanaka, one of Japan's best naval strategist, is giving instructions to his navy force: "Men we expect an American task force to hit us tonight. I think we can beat the Americans if we wait for them to start firing. By all means, don't use any searchlights. We'll be sitting ducks if you do. Just wait until they start firing and they will be good targets for our torpedoes. Let's hit them with everything we've got or else we're lost.

The Sailor & The Miracle Ship

Just after nightfall of November 30, orders came down from Admiral Wright to Task Force 67 to assume battle formation and enter Lengo Channel. The sister ship of the New Orleans, the heavy cruiser, U.S.S. Minneapolis was the flagship to lead the way. On the bridge of the New Orleans, Commander Oliver F. Naquin navigated the vessel. Captain C. H. Roper was in command and took charge. Naquin, a New Orleans man himself, had survived the sinking of the submarine Squlas and the hell aboard the battleship California in Pearl Harbor. On this night he was going to need all the luck and resourcefulness that had brought him through those two disasters. Tonight was going to be the worst.

The men went to their battle stations as the night watch started with the sound of eight bells. Suddenly the enemy was sighted off the port bow of the New Orleans. They were close inshore to Guadalcanal and not far from

The Sailor & The Miracle Ship

Savo and Florida Islands. For almost a half an hour the two units steamed toward each other. Then at 11:19 the America Task Force Commander, Rear Admiral Carlton H. Wright, gave the fire order and thirty seconds later an American destroyer let go a salvo. Thirty seconds later the Minneapolis first salvo was away. At 11:21 the main battery of the New Orleans, which had been loaded and ready, blasted nine shells to port and almost at that same instant, the Pensacola fired. Chief Signalman Harry C. Eaton, a boy from Tulsa, watched the red spots of tracer ends fading into the blackness of the night. The nineteen shells hit a Jap Cruiser all at the same time. Then there was nothing left. Commander W. F. Riggs, Jr., the Executive Officer, smiled grimly in "Batt Two" the after control station where he was in command. The guns quickly shifted to the second target, a destroyer. It quickly vanished. The American gun roared again and far away

The Sailor & The Miracle Ship

toward the island there was a terrific flash and explosion as an ammunition ship went the way of the cruiser and destroyer.

At 11:27 Naquin, by the flashes of his own guns saw a ball of fire envelope the Minneapolis. "She's gone," he thought. "Hard right rudder," he ordered his helmsman. This was to prevent ramming the slowing cruiser ahead. The New Orleans swung out of line to eastward. She was still swinging thirty seconds later when the Jap torpedo hit.

The ship had been in action a few minutes firing salvo after salvo from her big 8 inch guns. The torpedo exploded on the port side between Turrets one and two. This set off the magazines and they, in turn, set off seven thousand gallons of aviation fuel. Three explosions, merged into one, blew off the entire bow of the New Orleans, about a quarter of the ship's length. Turret two, just aft the break, jammed with it's guns trained outboard.

The Sailor & The Miracle Ship

All of it's men died instantly. Steering and engine controls from the pilot house went dead. The after control station took over.

Pete Edwards and crew were at their station ready to fire their guns when they were shaken by the tremendous jolt of the explosions.

"Boys, I don't know what happened," Edwards said. "But it ain't good. We've been hit and hit hard."

The dismembered bow still floated and as the ship continued to swing, it's momentum carried it aft, it's three guns pointing skyward. Seconds later, the bow crashed into the port quarter of the New Orleans, denting the plates and crippling the inboard propeller. "That's the first time a ship ever rammed herself," Naquin said to the men on the bridge.

Viewing from aft, the triple explosion looked like the end of everything. Sparks and fire shot far above the

The Sailor & The Miracle Ship

foremast. A column of water had drenched the ship. She rocked like a loping horse. But another torpedo was spotted off the starboard quarter. The New Orleans swung to port and the torpedo slid harmlessly by.

Severed completely from the ship, the bow slowly sank and disappeared beneath the surface of an angry sea. Only thin bulkheads just forward of Turret two held back the ocean. The ship was running forward, down twenty feet by the head, with water 4 ½ feet deep over her main deck. Her speed was two knots. She was almost unmanageable, and steering had to be done by the three remaining propellers. One hundred and seventy eight men were dead, dying or missing and twenty-three were injured.

Since "sick bay" was in the forward part of the ship, the few men that were in there were killed including

The Sailor & The Miracle Ship

Lieutenant Edward E. Evans of Portland, Oregon. The Forward Repair Party was also wiped out.

Due to the skill of the officers and crew, within two minutes after the explosions, the ship was under control again and headed for Tulagi at five knots, steering wildly, half sinking, afire, and still fighting with only one third of her main battery and three quarters of hull that still remained. Five minutes later Captain Roper was informed that a Japanese destroyer had been sighted. At the Captain's command, five and eight inch salvos were fired at the destroyer. The enemy ship turned tail and ran, and fortunate for the New Orleans. She could not have stood another hit. For about a half an hour she staggered on the flared-out plates and dangling keel holding her back and causing the ship to yaw wildly. For a time Edwards and the sailors back aft didn't know the details of just what had happened. Since Edwards was way down in the bottom of

The Sailor & The Miracle Ship

Turret three in the powder room, he didn't have a clue as to what was going on. When the powerful triple blast hit he was holding a 55 pound bag of powder in his arms. The concussion from the blast knocked him against the bulkhead, almost causing him to drop the bag of powder. Then word came over the public address system to prepare to abandon ship. Later the order was canceled. Then the men were served sandwiches and coffee.

Lieutenant Francis E. Malley of New York was in charge of the after repair party. When he went forward into the deep blackness of the ship, looking for the hole, suddenly, he stopped because it was a clear night and the stars were shining in his eyes. One more step and he would have fallen into the sea.

"Where's the bow?" he shouted.

"Gone, I guess," said Ensign John A. Zehner, who was then a boatswain and deck repair man. Zehner was very knowledgeable about most anything that had to do with seamanship.

The repair parties now went to work, first closing the watertight doors that had been sprung by the explosions. They worked with improvised diving masks made from gas masks. The bulkheads were holding, but for how long no one knew. Some of the heavy steel plates had been twisted like paper.

Five minutes after midnight as the New Orleans wallowed toward the harbor at Florida Island, suddenly, a Japanese searchlight beam swung toward her. She painfully turned north and barely avoided it. It looked scary for a few minutes but the searchlights never found that crippled, gallant ship. Then the message came from the repair party that the forward bulkheads were sagging. Captain Naquin reversed the engines and tried to get weight on the ship's stern to relieve the strain. When this failed, the ship wouldn't steer.

Before the explosions, the engines were running about 200 revolutions. They stopped suddenly and then started again. At this moment much of the machinery turned a deep blue. When tested later, it turned out that everything was in working order.

The Sailor & The Miracle Ship

The U.S.S. New Orleans with her bow and 120 feet of length blown off by a Japanese Torpedo.

❧ 8 ❧

Captain Roper called the crew together on deck for a meeting:

"Men, it goes without saying, we've been hit hard. Lost the bow and about one fourth the length of our ship. It looks like we were hit with about a 21 inch surface torpedo. It struck us between Turret 1 and Turret 2. We suffered three powerful explosions. The torpedo hit our port side exploding our magazines. Those two explosions tore off our bow. The third explosion was our aviation fuel which completely severed the bow which was hanging. The third explosion was a blessing. Otherwise we and the rest of the ship would have sunk with the bow. I'm telling you this to let you know that our ship might now survive. But we're gonna try to save her. However, the Honolulu was not hit. If any of you men want to transfer, you have my permission. It won't be held against you. Any questions or comments?"

The Sailor & The Miracle Ship

Edwards raised his hand.

"Yes, Seaman Edwards."

"Captain, I don't know about the rest of the men, but I'll stay with you and the ship."

"Aye, Aye," shouted the crew in unison.

"Men, you're a top-notch crew and I want you to know I'm proud of you and grateful to you. Something else, we've lost over 200 men and many of them are in Turret 2. I'm calling for volunteers to recover the bodies so we can get them off the ship."

Several hands go up, the first being Pete Edwards.

"Thanks, men," Captain Roper said. "Edwards you're in charge of the operation."

Edwards assembles his crew.

"Men, I'll go in first and look over the situation."

He crawls into Turret 2 and comes out after a couple of minutes.

The Sailor & The Miracle Ship

"Sailors, it looks mighty bad in there. The odor of burning flesh is awful. Due to the heat of the explosions, the skin of the dead is yellow like butter. We'll have to wear gas masks to get those men out. I'm telling you so any of you can back out of this job if you want to."

Nobody backs out. In spite of the gas masks, when they get inside the Turret and see the situation, two of the men throw up and two more pass out and have to be dragged out.

Edwards lays hold on to the arm of a body to pull him out and notices a tattoo of a heart with a dagger through the middle of the heart and the words M. L. Coyle, Spokane Washington. Edwards almost passes out at the realization that this is his buddy and the memory of the day he waited on him while he got the tattoo. Edwards could not hold back the tears and was glad he had on a gas

The Sailor & The Miracle Ship

mask so his shipmates couldn't see a seventeen year "Old Salt" crying.

There was much danger and much work yet ahead if the New Orleans was to be saved. There was no time for rest. This gallant, beat up, heavy cruiser, was defenseless. Two hundred of her crew were dead or wounded. She was open to Japanese air attacks. Somehow her bulkheads forward had to be shored up. If this could be accomplished, then she would have to sail 1700 miles to Sydney, Australia, the closest suitable repair facility. The two weeks voyage would provide the Japanese with ample time to finish the crippled cruiser off.

Slowly she was maneuvered across the harbor and up into a steaming jungle river, mooring her close to the bank and tying her to trees. A repair ship, the U.S.S. Maoussa, with a large crane, removed the three barrels from Turret 2. They lashed them down on the main deck

The Sailor & The Miracle Ship

aft (fantail) near Turret 3. Working parties were organized and seamen ashore became lumberjacks, cutting down trees and dragging them to cover and camouflage the ship. The branches were used for camouflage and the logs were used to shore up bulkhead 40, the most forward remaining bulkhead. If bulkhead 40 did not hold up underweigh the ship would sink. During the two weeks the ship was under temporary repair, frequently air raid alerts were sounded. Sometimes, three or four times a day the crew had to run back and forth between work and battle stations when alerts were sounded. When the Japanese tried to raid by air, the American marines on Guadalcanal would send planes up from Henderson Field and drive them off. The camouflage from stem to stern was so good that the Japanese planes could not spot the New Orleans.

Through Yankee ingenuity and Rebel tenacity, the New Orleans was given a coconut-log false face for her

The Sailor & The Miracle Ship

long journeys first to Sydney, Australia for a snub-nose bow, then to Puget Sound Naval Yards at Bremerton, Washington to be fitted with a permanent bow.

9

In mid-December of 1942 the New Orleans got underweigh bound for Sydney, Australia, seventeen hundred miles journey. After about two hours at sea, Captain Roper called all the crew on deck to inform them of a decision he had made.

"Men, my staff and I talked the situation over and we've decided the risk is too great to move forward. If we travel forward we think bulkhead 40 will give way and you know if that happens we'll sink. If you men are willing to stay with us we've decided to try backing the ship to Sydney. You know, also, we're sitting ducks to any Jap planes or ships that might spot us. Under these conditions if any of you are not willing to stay with us, we'll return you to Guadalcanal and it won't be held against you. Since it's your lives I wanted to get your input. Whata you say men?"

The Sailor & The Miracle Ship

Edwards raised his hand to speak.

"Yes, Seaman Edwards, whata you have to say?"

"Captain, I saw a movie one time that inspired me to join the Navy. The name of the movie was, 'Don't give up the ship', I don't know about the rest of these men but I feel the same way about our ship, 'Don't give up the ship.'"

"Aye, Aye," was the resounding cry to a man.

"Thank you men, you're a loyal crew and I appreciate every one of you."

The crew of the New Orleans was saddened at the thought of leaving their dead and wounded at Tulagi but there was nothing else they could do. Their ship had to be repaired as soon as possible so they could get back into action. On that long seventeen hundred mile journey, their nerves were on edge, wondering if their bowless cruiser would hold up. When they finally made it they were not

The Sailor & The Miracle Ship

only edgy but bone tired. While they were in route, the temporary bow was being built at Sydney with anything available including Japanese steel - light rails, angle iron, etc. - they had captured at Tulagi. Meanwhile, details had been sent to Bremerton, Washington as to the plans for a permanent bow. As Rear Admiral Tafinder smoked his big corn-cob pipe in the Administration Building at Puget Sound, he was planning his work and working his plans to have a new bow for the New Orleans when she arrived. He had learned that the ship was one of several of the Astoria class. She had come out in 1934 from the Brooklyn Navy Yard. Admiral Tafinder called in Commander E. E. Sprung, a hull expert of the yard and informed him of the problem and the need. Sprung went to work and a few days later plans for the new bow had taken shape on the huge mold floor. Steel plates came into the yard. Workmen rolled up their sleeves and went to work and the

The Sailor & The Miracle Ship

first steel was laid in dry dock. Few people in the yard knew anything. The Navy simply called it the "Ordship Nine."

While the ship was in repair at Sydney, Pete and his friend Hemrick went together on liberty to see the town.

"I'm short on money," Hemrick said.

"Man, they tell me you don't need much money to have a good time in this town," Edwards said. Especially us Navy men. They think we're heroes."

"I saw some mighty good looking girls in that crowd yesterday," Hemrick said. "Let's pick up a couple and do the town."

"Suit me."

They hadn't been in town long when they found they didn't have to pick up girls, the girls picked them up. With two pretty girls to show them around they toured the town.

The Sailor & The Miracle Ship

"Let's grab a trolley," Edwards said.

"Good idea," Hemrick said, "Let's ride around and see the town."

"What's the fare?" Edwards asked, "We've got to watch our money."

"Forget it," one of the girls said. "It's only a penny. We'll pay the fare", as she pulled out of her purse four coins the size of an American half dollar.

They rode the trolley for a couple of hours, seeing the town and enjoying themselves.

"I'm hungry," Hemrick said. "Let's find a restaurant and eat."

"How high's the food here?" asked Edwards.

"You can get a good meal for thirty-five cents, American money," said one of the girls. "Don't worry, we'll pay for the food."

The Sailor & The Miracle Ship

They found a restaurant and enjoyed a meal of steak and eggs for thirty-five cents apiece.

They walked around town, seeing the sights and enjoying the company of the girls until evening drew near. They thanked the girls, kissed them goodbye and headed back to ship.

"The Aussies sure talk funny," Hemrick said.

"Yeah," Edwards said. "But you'd better not criticize their talk. They'll fight you over their brogue. I guess they think we talk funny, too."

"By the way," Hemrick said. "You seemed to get on well with your girl today. What about your girl back home you've been talking about. Is the Aussie girl as pretty as she is?"

"The Aussie girl is pretty, all right, and good company but nothing like Micki back home with those big brown eyes and blond hair. That girl's a knock-out. I'm gonna ask her to marry me when I get home on leave."

While in Sydney, another thing Pete Edwards learned about Aussie life is that a certain time each morning and afternoon, everything stopped for tea time. Even if the crane operator, working on repair of their ship, picked up a load, he would stop at tea time and leave his load suspended in mid-air.

"By March of '43, the New Orleans had been made sea-worthy and she was ready to sail to the good old USA to have a permanent bow installed.

With her snub-nose bow, looking like a pug-nose bull dog, the gallant cruiser began her long journey to the United States. She had three heavy guns, her secondary battery, and anti-aircraft battery. She could only make fifteen knots, but she sailed proudly with three Jap flags on her bridge from the ships she had sent to the bottom. The

The Sailor & The Miracle Ship

Japanese were still claiming they had sunk her with the Minneapolis and the Northhampton. Unfortunately they were right about the Northhampton, but the badly battered "Miracle Ship" and the "Minnie" lived to fight Japs again.

Slowly, stopping in route, the New Orleans made her way north and east and finally steamed past Cape Flattery and up Puget Sound into dry dock. And there was her new bow waiting for her with Admiral Tafinder and a crowd of yard workers.

No time was wasted. Off came the temporary bow and the New Orleans forged slowly ahead and fitted herself up against her new stem section - a replica of the bow that lay on the bottom off Savo Island, seventy-five hundred miles away.

Commander Tafinder checked it out and cussed a little bit because it was almost an eight of an inch off, then agreed it was not so bad considering how she had been

The Sailor & The Miracle Ship

beat up. In fact she was a better ship since the original had been an all rivet job. Now she was one fourth welded and even stronger.

But they were not through yet. Later her sister ship, Minneapolis, came into port in need of repairs. They lifted out her number 1 Turret and later a crane lowered it into the new bow of the New Orleans.

This is the story of a great lady of the seas that refused to go down for the count but lived to help win the victory and keep America free.

While the repair work was in progress the crew was given 30 day leaves.

The Sailor & The Miracle Ship

The U.S.S. New Orleans fitted with a temporary bow sails from Sydney, Australia to Puget Sound Navy Yard in Washington.

~ 10 ~

Pete took the blackball ferry across Puget Sound to Seattle to catch the train home. When he boarded the train, he only had two sandwiches, one apple and fifty cents. After he had taken his seat, a dignified middle-aged man took the seat beside him.

"How are you sailor?" the man asked, holding out his hand. "My name is John Holden, what's yours?"

"I'm Pete Edwards. I'm headed home on leave to Nashville, Tennessee."

"I've got a son in the Navy. Looks to be about your age."

"I'm just seventeen. I enlisted at sixteen."

"How'd you get in the Navy at sixteen, young man?"

"It was my life's dream to be a Navy man and I worried the daylights out of my mother until she signed for me. I fibbed about my age."

The Sailor & The Miracle Ship

"The news is out about a ship they called the Miracle Ship that was beaten up badly at Guadalcanal, but somehow managed to make it back to the states."

"That's my ship, the New Orleans. Our task force was beaten up by Japanese torpedoes. We lost our bow and 200 men. We're being repaired now at Puget Sound."

"Son, a whole nation is grateful to men like you. I only hope my son does us as proud as an old salt like you," the man said with a smile.

"I'm sure he'll do fine," Edwards said.

"What you got in that paper sack, sailor?"

"Just a couple sandwiches and an apple I brought along."

"The food's on me this trip," Mr. Holden said. "Every time the diner calls mealtime, you eat with me."

"Thank you, Mr. Holden, but I don't know how I can ever repay you."

The Sailor & The Miracle Ship

"Forget it sailor. Maybe someone will be nice to my son."

"When young Edwards arrived at Union Station in Nashville, he broke his half dollar to pay his five cent bus fare home.

Pete got off the city bus a block from his home. As he walked up the porch steps he shouted at the top of his voice, "Hey Mama, I'm home!"

His mother rushed to the door and when she saw her son for the first time in almost a year, she wept for joy as she embraced her only son.

"Come in son, Pete's mother said, "Suppers almost ready."

"Supper," Pete said. "What a good sound. I'm ready for some home cooking after these many months of navy chow."

The Sailor & The Miracle Ship

"Son, we've been mighty worried about you," she said. "We knew you were in the thick of things in the Pacific. We heard about one of our Navy Task Forces being beaten up at Guadalcanal. Your ship was in that battle, wasn't it?"

"Yes, my ship the New Orleans, was badly crippled. She's in dry dock on the west coast being repaired now. They're calling her the "Miracle Ship" that wouldn't sink. Say, where's Sis?"

"She's gone to a movie with her boyfriend," Mrs. Edwards replied. "She thinks she's in love."

"What about my girlfriend, Micki? How's she doing?"

"We don't have much contact with Micki," Mrs. Edwards replied. "She's still in East High, a cheerleader."

"I'm gonna ask that girl to marry me," Pete said.

The Sailor & The Miracle Ship

"Pete, ya'll are too young to marry," Mrs. Edwards said, with a shocked look on her face. "At least wait'll you get out of the Navy. That'll be plenty of time to get married."

"I didn't mean right now, Mama. We'll wait a couple of years, but I'll ask her and let her be thinking about it."

Sis comes in and she and Pete embrace. They enjoy supper as they reminisce about old times.

"Sis when have you seen Micki?"

"Saw her yesterday at school, Pete. She said you wrote and told her you were coming home on leave soon. Said she was anxious to see you."

"That's my girl, she saving herself for me."

"I don't know about that, Pete," Sis said with a grin. "She's been dating another boy or two since you've been gone. Said she'd like to play the field."

The Sailor & The Miracle Ship

"She's just playing hard to get. I'll get that straightened out while I'm here. In fact, I'll call her tomorrow and set up a date. Well, I think I'll hit the sack, I've had a long hard trip." As Pete heads for bed the phone rings and Mrs. Edwards answers.

"Edward's residence. Mrs. Edwards speaking."

"Mrs. Edwards, this is Micki. I heard that Pete is coming home on leave, when is he due in?"

"As a matter of fact, Micki, he's here now. Said he was gonna call you tomorrow."

"May I speak to him, please?"

"Pete, it's for you," Mrs. Edwards said. "Micki wants to speak to you."

Pete takes the phone. "Hello Micki, how you doing?"

"Fine Pete. Good to hear your voice."

The Sailor & The Miracle Ship

"Same here. Let's get together tomorrow."

"Fine with me. What about Lucille's Restaurant for supper tomorrow?"

"That'll be fine. Then let's take in a movie at the Ritz."

"Sounds great. I can't wait to see you."

"I've got a very important question to ask you Micki, but it can wait."

"Ask me now Pete. Don't keep me in suspense."

"No, this is not the time and place. We need to be alone for this question."

"Okay, if you say so. See you tomorrow evening. Bye, bye for now."

Pete spent a restless night dreaming about that terrible battle in Lengo Channel. He could still feel the explosions on the New Orleans and hear the screams of wounded and dying sailors. At one time he woke himself up yelling. His mother came to his room. "Son, what's wrong?"

"Aw, Mama, I just had a dream about that battle we were in at Guadalcanal."

Mrs. Edwards sat on the bedside and cradled Pete's head much as she had done when he was a baby.

"Son, that was not a dream, that was a full-grown nightmare."

"I guess so Mama, but I'm okay now."

Mrs. Edwards continued to gently rock Pete until he dozed off.

The following evening Pete and his girlfriend got together for dinner and a movie.

"You look great in your uniform," Micki said.

"Hey, you're the one that looks great. "Never saw you look better. Miss me?"

The Sailor & The Miracle Ship

"Sure I missed you. Couldn't you tell it from my letters?"

"Yeah, I guess so. But there's a question I want to ask you."

"You mentioned that last night. What's the question?"

"Well, I'll be discharged in another two and a half years. Let's get married when I get out. How 'bout that?"

Micki fidgeted with her necklace, not knowing exactly what to say.

"Take your time," Pete said, as he drew her close and kissed her.

"This hit me sudden like Pete. I think we need to give that decision some time."

Pete was disappointed with her answer, almost to the point of saying something in anger but thought better.

The Sailor & The Miracle Ship

"You're right," he said. "But think about it and maybe you can give me an answer before I leave."

"I will, Pete. I'll put some serious thought on it," as she cuddled up to him.

Pete and Micki were together a lot during his leave but he never got a favorable answer concerning his proposal.

The days of Pete's leave flew by quickly. Although he was "salty" and hardened by battle at only seventeen, his mother still looked on him as her baby boy. She drove him to Union Station in Nashville to catch his train.

Mrs. Edwards walked with him to the train. "Now Mama, you turn around and walk back to the car and don't look back," Pete said as he kissed her goodbye.

"I don't think I can do that, son. Let me stay here and see you off."

The Sailor & The Miracle Ship

"No, Mama, it'll be easier if you just walk back to the car and go on home. I'm gonna get on that train and eat me an apple and everything will be okay," Pete forced a smile.

Mrs. Edwards cried all the way back home.

The Sailor & The Miracle Ship

11

Edwards made that long trip back to Bremerton, Washington to join the fleet. When he reported for duty Captain Roper gathered the men around him for instruction. He pointed to the dock where several of his men were standing who had returned late from their leaves, some of them several days late.

The voice of Captain Roper came over the public address system. Men, you have been wondering what happened to some of your shipmates. Well, there they are down on the dock. Some came in voluntarily, some were caught and brought in by M.P.'s. What do you think we ought to do with them?"

The sailors mumbled among themselves. "Well, I'll tell you what we're gonna do," Captain Roper said. "I want all of you to welcome them back and act as though they had never been gone."

The Sailor & The Miracle Ship

Captain Roper was a former enlisted man and had come up through the ranks. He was what they called a "Mustang." He knew his sailors that had overstayed their leave were well experienced regular Navy men and were in the Navy long before Pearl Harbor and that he needed these men to help win the war. Roper was the kind of leader who tempered justice with mercy. He was kind and considerate and knew how to get the best out of his men.

Shortly after Edwards returned to the fleet, his ship the heavy cruiser, New Orleans, was ordered to take part in bombarding Wake Island. His battle station had been the magazine of the lower powder handling room. He was transferred to the shell deck one level up where the projectiles were stored. Edward's duty was a shell hoistman. There were three shell hoists and three men to operate the hoists. During this raid on Wake Island they used projectiles weighing 260 pounds each.

The Sailor & The Miracle Ship

As the bombardment proceeded, being near the equator and handling 260 pound projectiles, the men were soaked with sweat and slowing down the pace.

Pete Edwards made a quick little pep speech.

"Men you know we were near losing this war and losing our country when the Japs hit Pearl Harbor. Had they followed up their advantage we might well have lost. Now we're on the move. We've rebuilt our Navy to the greatest in the world. We have the momentum. It's important that we take these islands back. Let's do our part to hit Wake and hit it hard so our Marines can take this island back."

With that the men got a new spurt of energy and fired all the shells on the lower level of the shell deck and started using the projectiles on the upper level. This was 3 ½ feet above the shell deck. To lower the projectiles to the shell deck they used a devise called a cradle. When the

The Sailor & The Miracle Ship

bombardment was over, there was not a dry thread on Edwards or any of his fellow sailors. Yes, Edwards was an "Old Salt" at the age of seventeen. But there was much more to be done to win the war, and dangerous times ahead for young Edwards.

In early 1943 the "Miracle Ship" New Orleans set sail for the Gilbert Islands to take part in the invasion. One day before the attack Edward's task force split into two units, one to raid Tarawa and the other Makin Island. The New Orleans attacked Makin Island. They hit the Gilberts so hard and so devastating was the attack that the Gilberts were no longer a threat.

By grapevine, word spread through the men of the New Orleans that their next operation would be to raid the Marshall Islands. Edwards felt, as did other crew members with whom he talked, that surely they would go to Pearl Harbor to restock. But it didn't work out that way.

The Sailor & The Miracle Ship

The order came down to Captain Roper that refueling would be done at sea.

Edwards thought to himself, "What in the world does a seventeen year old sailor know about refueling at sea?" He now appreciated the wisdom of Captain Roper's treatment of the many sailors who returned late to Puget Sound from leave. It would take salty men like they were to do a job like refueling at sea. So rather than to throw these men in the brig he came up with a mixture of mercy, justice and common sense. Edwards also thought how different the outcome would have been back at Guadalcanal had Captain Roper been in command of the American fleet that was demolished there and how many hundreds of lives would have been saved and the ships that would have been spared had Captain Roper been in charge.

The Sailor & The Miracle Ship

The New Orleans joined the task force and hit the Marshalls so hard that they like the Gilberts were no longer a threat. However, they patrolled the Islands a couple of days afterwards to intercept any possible Japanese ships that might show up. Within two months the New Orleans along with the rest of their fleet, had demolished the enemy installations.

～ 12 ～

Early December, 1943 the New Orleans docked at Pearl Harbor. Word came down on the P.A. system that Captain Roper wanted all men on the upper deck.

Edwards wondered, "What's this all about? Will we get orders for a new mission?"

The men gathered on deck and Roper began to speak: "Men you've served well. Because of men like you we've got the Japs on the run and there's light at the end of the tunnel. That does not mean the war is over. Much work yet to be done. Maybe another year or two. But we can't afford to let up. The harder we push and the harder we fight, the sooner we'll be going home for good. But for now, it's near Christmas, and I'm giving all you men Christmas leave except a skeleton crew. Get your leave papers today and you can depart for home tomorrow."

The Sailor & The Miracle Ship

Simultaneously, the men let out a loud cheer. "Wait," Captain Roper said. "I'm not through. Let this be a warning. Don't come back late from leave like many of you did at Bremerton. You won't get off as light."

At home on Christmas leave, Edwards recalled how different it was from Christmas a year ago in Australia, and how the seasons were the very opposite to the seasons in America. It was a strange thing to see people decorating Christmas trees in summer in Australia. Christmas leave for Edwards went by all too soon. He didn't see much of Micki. It seemed their relationship was in the cooling process, let alone any thoughts of marriage. After a long train ride west, he reported to the receiving station at Treasure Island, San Francisco.

≈ 13 ≈

On Easter Sunday, 1944, Pete Edwards was assigned to the newly commissioned Kaiser built aircraft carrier U.S.S. Cape Esperance, C.U.E. 88 at Astoria, Oregon. The mission of this "baby" flattop was to transport planes to firstline aircraft carriers. It's namesake was Cape Esperance in the Solomon Islands. This ship did not have a flight squadron for combat missions. The ship would load planes at certain points in the Pacific and fly them off to various front line carriers as needed. Pilots were brought in on destroyers to fly the planes to the carriers. They would rig a provision high line called a whit from the Cape Esperance to the destroyers when they pulled alongside with the pilots. The pilot sat in a canvas chair and was pulled over to the receiving ship. To have a little fun, Pete and some of the men hauling the pilots over would "accidentally on purpose" let too much slack in the line and let the pilot fall in the "drink." When

The Sailor & The Miracle Ship

the pilot was hauled out he would come up cussing and slinging water. It was all the sailors, looking on, could do to subdue their laughter to a snigger.

Captain Julian Brodus was commander of the Cape Esperance and Pete soon sized him up to be an overbearing, have my way or bust, kind of man and he had good reason for that opinion. While in port, Edwards was Coxwain of a 26 foot motor whale boat used to transport officers and crew members to various places. One evening while Edwards was eating supper, word came over the public address system, "Coxwain Benjamin Pete Edwards, lay up to quarter deck." Pete made his way to quarter deck and found the captain waiting for him.

"Edwards, take me to officers landing," he barked, with an expression like he'd just eaten a green persimmon.

"Aye, aye Sir."

The Sailor & The Miracle Ship

"Coxwain, square that hat and button those buttons," Brodus said with a scowl on his face.

"Aye, aye Sir." Edwards said as he saluted. "I was having supper when I got your call and didn't have time to get ship shape."

"Excuses won't do sailor. Let's get going."

It was windy when they made their way out to open harbor.

The captain gave the order to slow down.

Edwards sounded two bells which meant reduce speed. Captain Brodus proceeded to light a cigarette.

"Captain, don't do that. It's a hazard and against orders," Edwards shouted.

"Sailor," the captain said. "See that scow," as he pointed back to his ship. "I'm the captain of that ship and I give the orders around here."

The Sailor & The Miracle Ship

"Yes sir," Edwards said. "You're the captain of that ship but I'm in charge of this whale boat and I say, put out that cigarette."

Brodus ground out his cigarette angrily and shouted, "I'll see you later."

No more words were exchanged between Edwards and the captain until they reached the officers landing. As Brodus got off he looked back at Edwards. "Just remember what I said Coxwain. I'll see you later."

"Aye, aye Sir."

Later that evening Coxwain Edwards returned to the officers landing to bring Captain Brodus back to the ship. As the captain approached the boat he was staggering all over the place.

Edwards thought, "Why, he's as drunk as Cootie Brown."

The Sailor & The Miracle Ship

He managed by a struggle to get the captain on board. As they were pulling into the ship for a landing the captain stepped off too quickly and landed with a splash in the bay. They lowered the bow hook and lifted him on deck. The captain was shivering from the cold but managed an angry look at Edwards. "You better watch yourself or you'll be in the brig," he said.

From that night on it seemed that Captain Brodus had a grudge against Edwards and was out to get him.

A few days later Edwards was painting the sponson decks (small decks on the edge of the ship) when he saw a pair of tan shoes and khaki pantlegs. Edwards looked up and saw Captain Brodus looking down at him with a smirk on his face.

"Sailor, you'd better look out. I've got my eye on you. Be careful or you might wind up in the brig."

The Sailor & The Miracle Ship

"Captain, if you've got a complaint against me, tell me what it is. If it's about me asking you to put out that cigarette on the whale boat, I was just reminding you that smoking on that boat is a fire hazard and against regulations."

"Don't talk back, sailor. Just be on your toes. I'm watching you. Now get back to work."

"Aye, aye sir."

A favorite pastime of some of the sailors on ship was shooting dice. One night Pete and some of his buddies had a little crap game going. Pete had a streak of luck and won a little money when one of the men looked around and spied that pair of tan shoes and Captain Brodus standing looking down on them.

"Men, I'm confiscating this crap game money for the ship's welfare fund."

Edwards thought, "Yeah, welfare fund. That money'll go into his pocket." But he didn't say anything.

"Furthermore, if one of you objects I'll put every one of you on report. Any objections?"

For obvious reasons, nobody objected.

The Sailor & The Miracle Ship

Seaman Edwards and C. M. Green in front of
plane in the Philippines.

14

On December 18, 1944, the Cape Esperance was in the South China Sea loaded with planes to be delivered to combat Flattops. They had been given plenty of advance notice that they were on a collision course with a powerful typhoon. For some strange reason, unknown to this day, Captain Julian Brodus ignored the warning and headed straight into the typhoon. Second in command was Captain John Ballard who approached Captain Brodus about the course they were taking.

"Captain Brodus, if we head into that typhoon we're in grave danger of not only losing our planes but our ship and the three destroyers escorting us. Worst of all, by far, we're in danger of losing the lives of our men."

"Ballard, who is in charge of this ship?"

"You are captain. But why not skirt around the typhoon? It's not so urgent that we make time at the expense of so much possible and even probable loss."

The Sailor & The Miracle Ship

"Stay on course, Captain it's straight ahead."

"Very well, Captain, but I'm lodging an official complaint here and now and I'll put it on record."

Captain Brodus turned red faced but said nothing.

Headlong into a devil typhoon is an understatement in describing the destruction that typhoon dealt to the noble transport Carrier Cape Esperance. As they moved into the mouth of the typhoon, Edward's Jr. Division Officer Pierre Charbonnet approached him:

"Edwards, you take the wheel. You've had experience handling the wheel in rough seas. It's gonna be all we can do to make it through this devil in one piece. By all means you hold to that wheel and don't release it to anyone unless I tell you to."

"Aye, aye sir," Edwards said with a sharp salute.

They were now into the violent circle of the typhoon and Edwards was struggling to keep the ship on course.

The Sailor & The Miracle Ship

As a mighty wave rocked the ship, he heard a loud noise and looked around just in time to see dozens of airplanes sliding in unison toward the edge of the ship. The pressure had snapped the ropes that tied the planes to the deck. Edwards hoped against hope that the ship would right itself sufficiently to save the planes, but to no avail. He felt a surge of both sadness and anger as he watched the planes dump into the raging sea. The sadness was for the lost planes and the anger was toward Captain Brodus who had foolishly commanded that they proceed through that devilish killer typhoon in spite of all warnings not to do so.

At that instant Edwards felt a hand on his shoulder. It was Captain Brodus. He reached and took hold on the wheel and said in his condescending way, "Sailor, get out of the way. The way you're handling this wheel we're gonna lose this ship."

The Sailor & The Miracle Ship

"Captain," Edwards said. "You move out of the way. I have orders to hold this wheel regardless."

"Well, I'm commanding this ship and I'm giving you another command. Get out of my way."

Edwards thought about possible consequence for refusing the Captain's order but shoved him aside and took back the wheel.

As Brodus moved away, he shouted, "Edwards, I'll see that you're court marshalled for this."

"Do what you have to do Captain, but I'm trying to save this ship."

As Pete Edwards thought about all the planes lost overboard and the ones still on board that were being banged about, he thought, "It's good the planes were tied with ropes instead of cables, else we would have surely capsized with such a shift in weight."

The Sailor & The Miracle Ship

For four savage hours, the Cape Esperance battled her way through the raging raves of that typhoon tossed South China Seas to smoother sailing.

Captain Brodus called John Ballard, his second in command, to his quarters for an evaluation of their losses.

"Ballard we've been through some rough times. What's your estimation of damage?"

"Well, Captain, you remember I told you not to take us into that typhoon. To put it mildly, it was a needless, foolish decision."

Pounding his desk with his fist, his face red with rage. "Just give me a rough estimate of the losses. That's all I want from you," Brodus yelled.

"Well, I've taken a quick survey and most of our planes have gone overboard. The few of the original sixty-five left on deck are so battered and beat up we'll have to throw them overboard. All three of our escorting

The Sailor & The Miracle Ship

destroyers, Monihan, Spence and Hull, were sunk. We lost a lot of good men on those destroyers. We got word from some of those we managed to rescue that they ran out of fuel and without fuel were powerless to stay afloat. It's worse than bad, Brodus, and you're to blame."

Brodus arose from his desk with clenched fists as though he wanted to hit Ballard but thought better and dismissed him.

The Cape Esperance headed back to the states and made port in Vallejo, California in early January, 1945. It was obvious the news about the Cape Esperance, and the losses suffered in the typhoon had reached Naval headquarters. Special agents came aboard the ship to question Captain Brodus.

"Captain, it has been reported to us that you made the decision to sail into that typhoon in spite of the fact you had been given advance warning that it was a powerful typhoon."

"Yes, I gave the order. And who do you think you are to come aboard my ship to question me?"

The agents presented their gold badges and identified themselves. Captain Julian Brodus was relieved of his command but obviously not soon enough.

The Sailor & The Miracle Ship

≈ 15 ≈

In mid January, 1945, Pete Edwards was granted leave. When he got off the plane in Nashville and walked into the airport there was a spirit of cheer among the people. He soon learned the reason for the apparent happiness. It was because of the optimism in the newspapers and on radio that the war would soon be over and many loved ones who had fought so gallantly for liberty would soon be coming home. Of course there was sadness that many who had died for freedom would not be returning. But the overall mood was one of happy anticipation of the war's end. Pete spotted his mother and sister in the waiting area. They greeted him with hugs and tears of joy — picked up his luggage and made their way to the car. The first mile or so on the way home not much was said as they silently savored the precious moments together. Pete broke the silence:

The Sailor & The Miracle Ship

"Mama, you know how much I like music and how much I like to sing. I've always associated certain songs to certain times and events and when I hear those songs it brings vividly to my mind certain things and when those things happened."

"Yes, son, I know your love for music and if I do say so, you're a good singer."

"On the way home, somebody near me had a small battery radio. Some of the songs I heard were *"Rum and Coke"* by the Andrew Sisters, *"Accentuate the Positive"* by Johnny Mercer and Doris Day's smash hit *"Sentimental Journey"*. Even now when I hear Bob Wills record *"San Antonia Rose"*, it brings sharply to my mind September 1, 1939, when German troops invaded Poland. I know the hits of today will rekindle memories of my active navy career every time I hear those songs.

The Sailor & The Miracle Ship

All too soon it was drawing toward mid February and the days of Edwards' leave were winding down. He and his mother are in the kitchen having supper.

"Mama, I've got the sore throat and it hurts to swallow my food."

"Son, get you a glass, fill it with warm water, put a half teaspoon of salt in it, stir it up and gargle several times."

Pete complied with his mother's instructions.

"Did that help your throat, son?"

"A little Mama, but not much. But I've got to finish packing. My train leaves Union Station at seven and it's already five-thirty."

Edwards didn't have the money to ride Pullman and had to sleep in the lounge. He went to sleep about 9:00 o'clock and woke up about 11:30. He looked in the mirror and saw both sides of his jaws swollen and looking

The Sailor & The Miracle Ship

like he had a big candy jaw-breaker in each side. The train stopped at Evansville, Indiana. Two shore patrol came to question Pete.

"Sailor, where are you headed?" one of the men asked.

"Treasure Island," Pete answered.

"You don't look too sick to me," one of the Patrolmen said. "You'll make that in a breeze."

"Hold on," the other man, a Chief Petty Officer, said. "The kid's too sick to make that trip. We're taking him to the hospital."

"Let me see your leave papers, sailor," the doctor said as he took a look at Pete and slid his papers in his desk drawer.

"Doctor, I have to have my leave papers back."

"When you leave the hospital you'll be issued a new set. Mate, you'll be here for a while. You've got the mumps." During his stay in the hospital his mother visited him. They went to a restaurant one night. Pete played the record, *"You've Got To Accent The Positive."* He was leaning on the juke-box and singing along. His mother was young looking for her age — pretty and a sharp dresser. There were two girls sitting near her table, admiring this young sailor and his singing. "That young sailor is good looking and a good singer," one of the girls said. "I want to meet him."

"You'd better be quiet," said the other girl glancing at Mrs. Edwards. "That's his wife over at that table."

Mrs. Edwards overheard their conversation:

"No, I'm not his wife," she said. "I'm his mother."

The Sailor & The Miracle Ship

Seaman Edwards in front of plane.

~ 16 ~

Edwards was discharged from the hospital on March 24 and set his course for Treasure Island, San Francisco. He then boarded a troop transport so crowded that they had to stand to eat their meals. The passengers got only two meals a day and had to take salt water showers. Edwards learned that mess cooks ate three times a day and had fresh water showers so he volunteered as a mess cook. Enroute to the Philippines, Edwards fared well including three meals a day and fresh water showers. In transit he made friends with a yeoman. As a mess cook at times he would slip food to the yeoman, who, in turn, used his influence to get Edwards assigned to Naval Shore Facilities 3964 on the island of Samar in the Philippines, a base operated by the Sea Bees, across San Pedro Bay from Taelobin, Leyte. Pete Edwards liked land based duty. To him it was like a vacation compared to ship duty. The mission of the base was the repair and upkeep of all types

The Sailor & The Miracle Ship

of small craft. They would pull the boats out of the water on to a sand covered slab to be inspected. One day they pulled an L.C.V.P. (Landing Craft Vehicle Personnel) that was practically new. Edwards wanted that craft for their personal use. He approached their Division Officer:

"Sir, I wish you'd survey that boat. I think it has worm holes."

"What you trying to pull Edwards? There's nothing wrong with that boat and you know it."

"I know it, Lieutenant Mills and that's the reason I want you to survey it."

"You know Edwards, you're a crafty cuss. You'd make a good lawyer."

They both had a good laugh and then Lieutenant Mills surveyed the boat. They had the boat painted and named it S-4. The "S" meant it had been surveyed so it could be listed with the Port Director as a means of

The Sailor & The Miracle Ship

identity. When Edwards and some of his friends wanted to take a ride they would back a jeep into the boat and when they got tired of sailing they would land, drive the jeep out and take a drive.

By this time Seaman Edwards had been advanced to Carpenter's Mate Third Class. On August 14, he was sitting in the outside movie area watching a movie called, "*A Metal for Benny.*" Since his name was Benjamin, he thought, "What a name for a movie!"

Edwards thoughts were drifting back and forth between home and the movie, hoping this war would soon be over so he could get back home. Suddenly someone shouted from the road, "The war is over." Edwards thought it was a joke and thought, "Yeah the war's over, all over the world." Within a minute he knew the end of the war had come when ships out on the harbor started

The Sailor & The Miracle Ship

blowing their whistles and firing their guns and rockets. Needless to say the movie was over and so was the war. Then Edwards remembered another war song he loved, *"When The Lights Go On Again All Over The World"* and a surge of joy filled his heart as he thought, "Now we've come through the darkness of war and indeed the lights will go on all over the world and how he hoped that never again would the world lapse back into the black night of war."

Now that the war was over, Pete Edwards was almost as anxious to get out of the navy as he was to get in. While waiting discharge, Edwards was assigned to the Navy Station in New Orleans, Louisiana as a guard at the Brig.

"Guard," one of the prisoners called to Pete one day.

The Sailor & The Miracle Ship

"What is it, sailor?" Edwards said as he drew near the cell door.

"Would you do me a favor?"

"If I can. What's the favor?"

"I'm doing time for being AWOL My mother lives here in New Orleans. She's a widow, trying to make ends meet by selling neck ties she makes. Would you visit her and tell her I'm okay and I'll be out of the Brig before long and I'll try to do better."

"Yeah, sailor. I'll be glad to visit your mother. What's your name?"

"Name's Chris Newman and my mom lives at 602 Piney Street."

The next day Edwards did visit Newman's mother. He found Piney Street and walked along the sidewalk on the even number side until he spotted the mailbox number 602. As he surveyed the small clapboard frame house with

113

The Sailor & The Miracle Ship

the mildewed shingles on the roof and the paint pealing on the clapboards, he felt compassion for this poor widow struggling to get by and her only son in the Brig. But he needn't have felt sorry for the dear lady because what he saw as she answered his knock was a bundle of good cheer and optimism in the sparkling eyes of this forty some odd pretty lady with her salt and pepper hair. Pete thought, "If she were only twenty years younger or I were twenty years older I could go for this lady."

When he told her his mission, she almost shouted with joy because he had brought her a message from her beloved son.

"My name's Mary Newman. Come in and tell me more about Chris. How's he doing? Is he well? How's he looking" The questions were coming in bunches.

Pete smiled and said, "I'll answer in order. Chris is doing well, his health is fine and he's looking good."

The Sailor & The Miracle Ship

Pete took a seat and glanced around the room. He saw a pedal type Singer sewing machine in one corner on which she sewed neck ties to sell. He saw three beautiful homemade ties hanging over the back of a chair.

"Beautiful ties," Pete said. "Chris told me you made ties for sale. I'd like to buy a couple."

"You can't buy 'em, but I'll give you a half a dozen. Pick you out six."

"No, can't do that. You put a lot of work into those ties and that's your business."

"No, don't say another word. They're your free gratis. What you've done for me in bringing me word from Chris is worth far more than a few neckties."

"Okay, thanks much. Tell me something about Chris. I just met him yesterday. What kind of a boy is he?"

The Sailor & The Miracle Ship

"Basically, Chris is a good boy in spite of his upbringing. Never had much of a chance in life. His dad was a woman chasing, alcoholic. He'd come home drinking and beat up on me and little Chris. When Chris was about fifteen he came home from school one day and his dad was beating me and threatening to kill me. Chris went and loaded his Dad's shotgun and when he came back and saw him chasing me with a butcher knife, he leveled down on him and killed him. The law came and later there was a hearing. They agreed it was justifiable homicide."

"You and Chris have had it pretty tough, huh?"

"I guess you could say that, but I'm not complaining. I've tried to do what I could to help Chris get his head on straight. He was serving at the Great Lakes Naval Base in Chicago. He got word I was sick and when he couldn't get leave, he went AWOL and came home to see about me. They caught him and put him in the Brig here in New Orleans."

"Well, he told me to tell you he'll be out of the brig in a couple of weeks and he'd be returned to his base in Chicago. He wanted me to tell you that he'd do better and serve his navy time out as a good sailor."

Pete picked him out six ties and headed for the door.

"Sailor, your visit has meant the world to me. Thanks so much. Tell Chris I love him and I'll be praying for his safe return home."

The Sailor & The Miracle Ship

Seaman Edwards on the U.S.S. Macon.

~ 17 ~

Pete Edwards was discharged from the Navy in New Orleans on June 5, 1946. He was standing tall in the Administration Building when the yeoman handed him his discharge making him a civilian again. He was now twenty-one years old having spent most of his active navy time as a minor. As his mind drifted back over the past 3 years, 9 months and 21 days of navy life and the dangerous times and close calls he'd come through, Pete Edwards thought, "Surely the Lord must have a reason for sparing me through perilous times. He must have a purpose for my future. I believe the best is yet to be. I'll try, with His help, to make the rest of my life the best of my life."

Little did Edwards realize what a great and exciting future he did have. One of the wisest decisions he ever made was to join the Naval Reserve on the very day he was discharged.

The Sailor & The Miracle Ship

After returning home things didn't go too well for Pete. Since about all he knew was navy life, it took him a while to get adjusted to civilian life. He spent his mustering out pay in nothing flat. For a while he didn't even apply himself in the Naval Reserve. Although he attended the Reserve drills he took little interest. But there were two people out there on the horizon of his future, destined to help him get his life straight.

~ 18 ~

Youth Awareness, a civic organization made up primarily of concerned parents, was sponsoring a dance for the young people. Pete wanted to go but he'd blown all his money and was too proud to go to the dance financially embarrassed. He mentioned his plight to his mother:

"Mama, I want to go to that dance at Cooper's Place on Saturday night but I'm broke. Could you lend me five dollars?"

"Now Pete, I've told you you need to get a job. You need to get your life organized. Use some of that discipline you learned in the navy."

"I know, Mama and I'm gonna settle down and go to work. But I do want to go to that dance. Will you let me have the money?"

"I'll think about it. Another thing, I don't like the idea of you going to a dance. In my young days, they used

The Sailor & The Miracle Ship

to have dances at first one house and the other and some of the boys would bring a jug of moonshine and get high and then start a fight."

"Mama, this dance is nothing like that. It will be sponsored by Youth Awareness and will be chaperoned by parents."

"I didn't know you could dance Pete. Where'd you learn to dance?"

"In the navy, Mama. I can jitterbug better than the jitterbug himself."

"Well, okay, I'll let you have the five dollars, but you're gonna have to start working and make your own money."

On the Saturday afternoon of the big dance, Pete left home at 5:30. He wanted to get to the dance before it got started so he could look the girls over as they came in. He and Micki had split up so he didn't have a regular girl to

The Sailor & The Miracle Ship

take to the dance. He walked to Woodland Street and caught a city bus to Cooper's Place in West Nashville. He was hoping to find a girl to dance with. He noticed as they came in most of the girls had dates. He looked around over the dance floor and spotted two girls who didn't seem to have escorts. As he walked toward them, his eyes zeroed in on one of them and he knew that was the girl for him not only for that night but for keeps.

"These are the most beautiful brown eyes I have ever seen" he thought. "And look how that brown hair highlights those eyes and frames that pretty face," he wondered, "Where has she been all my life?"

He approached her and introduced himself.

"I'm Benjamin Edwards," thinking the first part of his name sounded more dignified than Pete. "What's you name?"

The Sailor & The Miracle Ship

"I'm Aliene Collier. I had a date but he had to work overtime. Said he'd try to get here later."

"Where's your home?"

"I live in Adairville, Kentucky, just across the Tennessee-Kentucky line."

"What are you doing all the way down here in Nashville?"

"Oh, I'm going to Draughons Business College here in town."

"Would you dance with me?"

"I don't know if I should. My boyfriend is pretty jealous and I don't know how he'd take it if he caught me dancing with another boy. But I guess it's okay."

The band was made up of four of the WSM radio staff band that had formed to play dances. They were playing an upbeat version of Kay Kaiser's hit, "Three Little Fishes." The young couples were jitterbugging all over the place. But when Pete and Aliene hit the floor and got into their version of jitterbug which later was dubbed the "Twist," all the other dancers backed off to the side to watch them do their thing. They were roundly applauded when the band finished the number.

Then the band went into the *"Tennessee Waltz."* The crowd was still watching them as they glided over the floor with the grace of a swan lifting off a placid lake. As Pete caught a gentle whiff of Aliene's perfume he drew her even closer and he knew in his heart of hearts this would be the love of his life. They were oblivious to anyone else as they floated over the floor. Two thirds through the number, Pete felt a tap on his shoulder. It was Aliene's boyfriend cutting in. He not only cut in but he took Pete to task for dancing with his girl.

The Sailor & The Miracle Ship

"Listen buddy, you keep your hands off my girl and if you don't stay away from her I'll bust you one..."

"Joe Hinkle," Aliene said. "You shut your mouth. I don't belong to you and I can dance with anyone I please."

Hinkle slapped her and with one punch in the jaw, Pete flattened him.

"Would you walk me home?" Aliene asked Pete, with tears in her eyes. "I room just three blocks from here."

"Be glad to."

It was an early October night and there was a chill in the air. Pete removed his jacket and gently placed it around Aliene's shoulders.

"Thank you," Aliene said. "I apologize for the way Joe acted tonight. He seems to be a nice boy other than his jealousy and possessiveness and I learned tonight, I can't take that. I'm gonna break it off with him."

The Sailor & The Miracle Ship

"You don't owe me an apology. Had he just cut in and left it at that, that would have been okay. But when he made a scene and slapped you that was the last straw. I couldn't take that."

Pete put his arm around her shoulder and drew her closer. There was a bright October full moon and for a time they walked silently. Aliene broke the silence:

"Where do you live?"

"I live across the river in East Nashville."

"Where do you work?"

"Not working right now. Just discharged from the navy a short time ago and haven't found a job yet. What about you? How much more time before you get out of business school?"

"About another year and then I'll be going back home and take a job in Adairville."

The Sailor & The Miracle Ship

Pete thought, "Not if I can help it, you won't be going back to Kentucky. You'll be my wife within six months."

"I room right here," Aliene said, as they approached a two story brick house.

"You've been very nice," Aliene said. "Other than that fracas with Joe, I've enjoyed myself."

"Could I see you again?" Pete asked.

"I'd like that Benjamin. Stay in touch."

"Call me Pete. That's what most folks call me. I introduced myself to you as Benjamin, thinking that sounded more impressive. My first name is Benjamin, but if it's okay, just call me Pete."

"Good night," Aliene said as they approached the door.

The Sailor & The Miracle Ship

"It's already been a good night for me," Pete said. "Just being with you has made it a good night. I hope it's been a good night for you too."

"For the most part, it was enjoyable."

"Would you think I'm out of order if I asked you to let me kiss you goodnight?"

"I guess it's okay," Aliene said in a shy voice.

Pete drew her to him and gently kissed her on the lips and he sensed she was feeling the same emotion he was feeling.

All the way home on the city bus, Pete was on cloud nine. He slept very little that night, feeling some of the same excitement he had felt six years before on the night before he enlisted in the navy the next day.

He arose around seven the next morning and went into the kitchen where his mother was cooking breakfast. He smiled at her, hugged her and kissed her on the cheek.

The Sailor & The Miracle Ship

"Why are you so happy this morning, son?"

"You won't believe what happened last night, Mama. I met the girl of my dreams and believe me she is a dream girl."

"Aw, Pete, that's what you said about Micki and that didn't last. Don't get all worked up now."

"Mama, this is different. It's a different feeling from anything I've ever felt about a girl. Mama, you've heard of love at first sight. We'll that's what this is. I'm in love."

Mrs. Edwards smiled. "Take it easy Pete. Give yourself some time. You may get over this. You may even find a girl you like better."

"No Mama, I can feel it. This is the girl I want to spend the rest of my life with."

"Well, if you feel that way you'd better get out and get a job. Marriage is expensive."

The Sailor & The Miracle Ship

"I will, Mama. In fact, John Hutchins, a navy buddy of mine, shortly before we both were discharged, told me if I'd come to Lansing Michigan, his hometown, that he'd help me get a job. Said work was good there."

"Son, you mean you'd be willing to leave this new found girlfriend and go all the way to Michigan to work?"

"Mama, if I can get a job there and if she'll marry me, we can live in Lansing."

Next day, Sunday afternoon, Pete went to the rooming house where Aliene was living on the chance he'd find her there. As luck would have it, she was at home. They walked to Elliston Place Soda Shop for some ice cream and then much of the afternoon in beautiful Centennial Park, enjoying the company one of the other and the multicolored splendor of Autumn.

"Aliene, I know we just met last night, but I feel about you like I've never felt about another girl. Like I told

The Sailor & The Miracle Ship

my Mama, I think I'm in love. I don't know how you felt last night, but I believe you felt something special too."

Pete noticed that Aliene was nervous and didn't seem to know what to say.

"Take your time, Aliene and give it some thought."

"I will Pete. But I admit I've never had a feeling like this about another boy."

"I was thinking," Pete said with a serious look on his face. "Would there be a possibility that you would think about marrying me?"

"Things are moving too fast, Pete. We don't need to rush into this and maybe be sorry later. But I will think about it."

"That's all I ask. I've got a good chance at a job in Lansing, Michigan. Work is slack around here. I'll go to Lansing and try to get lined up with a job there."

The Sailor & The Miracle Ship

"I wish you could get a job in Nashville. Why don't you give it another week here and see if you can get a job?"

"Well, I'll try it this week, but if I don't get a job here, I'll head for Lansing. I've just got to go to work."

Pete hit it lucky and landed a job that week with Buchi Plumbing Company. Their love grew stronger as Pete and Aliene continued to see each other on a regular basis. Aliene was working at a part time job to help pay for her education. Pete continued on his job for about a year. He was not making much money and didn't see much of a chance for advancement. He contacted his navy buddy in Lansing to see what the chances were of getting a better paying job there. John Hutchins said there were plenty of jobs available there and the pay was good and insisted that Pete come up and give it a try. Pete decided to do that and informed Aliene of his decision.

The Sailor & The Miracle Ship

"Aliene, I've decided to go to Lansing and get a better paying job. But I want to ask you again, will you marry me?"

"I will Pete, but first go to Lansing and see if you can get a job. Meanwhile, I'll be through school in another week and I have a clerical job lined up. If you get a job, let's both work a while and save some money. We'll be needing furniture and other things that go with housekeeping. Let's wait a few months, then we can get married."

"Okay, but I'm gonna miss you something awful. I don't think there's any doubt that I'll get a job. I'll write you two or three times a week."

"You do that and I'll be sure to answer."

"I take it that our engagement is official. Right?"

"Yes Pete," Aliene said, misty eyed.

The Sailor & The Miracle Ship

Pete saw the tears in her eyes and knew these were tears of joy and not tears of hurt like he had seen when Joe Hinkle pitched a jealous fit and slapped her at the dance a year ago.

"I'll be leaving tomorrow," Pete said. "And won't be seeing you for a while but remember always, I love you."

"And I love you Pete."

They melted into each others arms with a prolonged kiss that sealed their engagement.

Pete and Aliene kept in touch by letter all the while he was working in Lansing. His first job was with R.I.O. Motor Company. He worked there until he was laid off. He then went to work for the Grand Trunk Railroad Company and worked there until there was a rail strike. He was getting homesick — most of all it was the "Lovesick Blues" to be with Aliene. He decided to come

The Sailor & The Miracle Ship

home and wait out the strike and then return to Lansing. He hoped that Aliene would be ready to get married. He rode the Greyhound bus to the bus station in Nashville and then caught a city bus to his home on Russell Street. He arrived home about 4:00 o'clock Friday afternoon and found his mother preparing supper.

"Son, I didn't know you were coming home. Glad to have you back home. Supper's about ready. Wash up and we'll eat. Sis'll be home from work any minute. Why'd you come home?"

"Aw, the job where I work is having a rail strike and I decided I'd come home and wait it out. Most of all I wanted to see you and Sis and Aliene. I'm gonna try to get Aliene to marry me while I'm here."

Pete phoned Aliene and they set up a meeting at 6:30 at Eliston Place Soda Shop. There they discussed wedding plans and decided to go to Rossville, Georgia the

The Sailor & The Miracle Ship

following Sunday and get married by a Justice of the Peace where there was no red tape.

The Sailor & The Miracle Ship

Benjamin P. (Pete) Edwards

~ 19 ~

January 11, 1948, was a cold, crisp, sunshiny morning when Pete, Aliene, his mother and a friend of Pete's mother loaded up in the car owned by Mrs. Edward's friend and headed to Rossville Georgia just across the state line from Chattanooga. There they found the house of a Justice of the Peace who performed the wedding ceremony for Pete and Aliene. Aliene did not have a wedding ring so Mrs. Edwards let her use her own wedding ring for the ceremony.

They drive back home to Nashville that afternoon. There was no time nor money for a honeymoon. They borrow Mrs. Edward's friend's car for the night and drive to a motel on Gallatin road and rent a room.

"Sweetheart," Pete said. "This is the best I can do for a honeymoon since you have to be back at work tomorrow morning, we're short on both time and money.

The Sailor & The Miracle Ship

At least this will be a night we'll remember and treasure the rest of our lives."

"Hon, that's okay," Aliene said. "Later we'll be able to go on a full fledged honeymoon."

Pete carries her over the threshold and gently lays her on the bed. They're both nervous and timid hardly knowing what to say or do.

"Pete, my Mama always told me to keep myself for my husband and I've done that and tonight I reckon I'm all yours, but please be gentle with me."

They dress for bed, turn out the lights and there as a bright January moon bathes their bed through a window, they drink deeply of the ecstasy and bliss that only a wedding night can bring.

Toward the latter part of the week Pete got word from his navy buddy in Lansing that the rail strike was over and that he should report for work the following

The Sailor & The Miracle Ship

Monday. He and Aliene were living for the time being with Mrs. Edwards.

He broke the news to Aliene. "Honey, I have to be back at work Monday morning. I'll go on back and get settled and get us a place to stay and then send for you. Will you come up?"

"Sure I will honey. Remember that scripture the Justice of the Peace read at our wedding, 'Whither thou goest, I will go?' Well, he was talking to me and that means you're my husband and where you go I'll go."

"I love you for that, sweetheart and I'll try to be a good husband. I'll care for you and protect you."

"Just let me know in plenty of time," Aliene said. "I'll have to give a week's notice on my job. I'll count the days looking for the time when we can be together again."

Pete returned to his job in Lansing. He later sent for Aliene. After spending considerable time there they

The Sailor & The Miracle Ship

decided to move back to Nashville so they would be closer to their kinfolk's and friends. Pete bought a new house on the GI Bill with no down payment and a 4 ½ percent loan. Another piece of good fortune for Pete and one of the best things that ever happened in his life, was the fact that one of his neighbors was a retired Master Chief Boatswain Mate. John R. Burton, Jr.. He was dedicated to making the Nashville Naval Reserve the best possible. Because of Chief Burton, they had more chiefs in his outfit than White Hats. He was a credit to the Navy and an inspiration to his men. His study methods, instruction and counseling was commended at the 6th and 8th Naval Districts. The word was out that "Chief Burton looks after his men like a mother hen looks after her baby chicks." It was due to the strong encouragement by Chief Burton that Edwards rejoined the Naval Reserve. When he came back to the Reserve, his rate was Steel Worker 3rd class. He passed

The Sailor & The Miracle Ship

three tests his first year back. One night during a drill, Chief Burton approached Edwards:

"Edwards, I want you to be the instructor of one of my classes."

"Chief, I don't know anything about instructing a Naval class."

"You'll do okay. The guy that's supposed to instruct tonight didn't show up. I'm in a spot. Take a quick look over this book of questions and you'll do fine."

Edwards did well and the next week Chief Burton gave him a class of his own. Edwards liked this more than anything he'd ever done in the navy.

Under the guidance of Chief Burton, Edwards became so good that two of his men made the highest test scores in the navy including both the regular and Reserve Navy. When this word came to the 6th Naval District at Charleston, South Carolina, they thought some hanky panky was going on in Nashville. So they sent a Naval Intelligence Officer to investigate the Nashville study methods. After the completion of the Intelligence Officer's investigation, he met with Chief Burton.

"Chief, after hearing of the high scoring over here, in all honesty, we felt there might be something shady about it. However, I find nothing wrong with this Reserve Center's study method. As a matter of fact, I find them to be highly commendable and I will encourage other Reserve Centers to use your system. You have about as many Chiefs here as you do white hats. How do you do it?"

"Thank you sir," Chief Burton said. "After a test for advancement has been given, I have the men that took the test meet with me in my basement at home. I get the men to write all the questions from the test they can remember.

The Sailor & The Miracle Ship

Questions I can't answer I look up the answers and keep them for future reference."

"A good idea, Chief. Even though your Reservist are at a disadvantage in competing with the men in full-time active duty, you're still scoring higher than the regulars. Thanks for your dedication and the extra time you put in to make the Nashville Reserve Center one of the best."

"Thank you, sir. We'll continue to do our best."

"Another thing, Chief. I've been hearing about the good work your Reserve is doing for needy children in giving them a Christmas party each year. I've heard you have a man, Chief Benjamin Edwards, who does a good job playing Santa Claus each year."

"That's right, Chief Burton said with a smile. "Chief Edwards has played Santa so much that he's come to believe he really is Santa Claus."

The Sailor & The Miracle Ship

Chief Edwards receiving an award in New Orleans.

20

Chief Benjamin Peter Edward's last two week tour of active duty of his Navy Reserve career was in the summer of 1978. He was assigned to Coastal River Division 22 at New Orleans, Louisiana, the headquarters of the 8th Navy District. As Edwards was checking in one of the men in the office heard him say he had served on this city's namesake. He asked Edwards if he was on the heavy cruiser New Orleans the night she was torpedoed.

"I'm sorry to say I was," Pete said with sadness in his voice.

"I work across the Mississippi," the sailor said. "I'll give you the Admiral's phone number because I know he'd sure like to talk with you."

"Sailor, I don't think I have much business calling an Admiral."

The Sailor & The Miracle Ship

Pete didn't think anymore about it until that evening in the dining hall.

He was eating when a Chief Petty Officer came to him and asked him, "Are you Chief Edwards?"

"Yes I am."

"The Admiral desires your presence in the morning at 0800 at headquarters. If I were you I'd be in my dress blues."

"Uh, oh," Pete thought. "What in the world have I done now?"

Edwards got up early the next morning and nervously showered and shaved, getting ready for his meeting with the Admiral. All the while he kept wondering what this was all about. After breakfast, he took a motor launch across the river to headquarters. He walked in the front office and was greeted by a Yeoman, who grabbed Pete's hand and shook it like he was a long lost brother.

"Will you have a seat Chief? The Admiral is expecting you and he will receive you shortly."

As Pete waited he was getting more nervous all the while.

Presently, the Yeoman approached him, "The Admiral will see you now Chief. You may go in."

It was one of the biggest surprises of his life when Chief Edwards walked in and saw the Vice-Admiral sitting at his large desk. He was looking at his former Jr. Division Officer, Lieutenant Jr. Grade who had served with him on the New Orleans. Only now he was looking at Vice-Admiral Pierre Charbonnet.

The Admiral stood up and held out his hand with a grin on his face. He looked at Edward's rating badge and service stripes.

The Sailor & The Miracle Ship

"Ed, it looks like you've done okay."

"Admiral, you haven't done so bad yourself. Those big silver stars on your collar almost put my eyes out when I walked in."

They both had a good laugh. Then they reminisced about that terrible night of November 30, 1942, thirty-six years ago when the New Orleans and all of the ships of the task force, except one, were either sunk or heavily damaged by a Japanese task force.

"Ed, did you know that the U.S.S. New Orleans was the most damaged ship of World War II not to sink? As a matter of fact, some of the ships with much less damage than ours did sink." The New Orleans is now dubbed 'The Miracle Ship'."

"Yes, Admiral, and the credit goes to our superior captain, Captain Clifford Roper and the super crew we had including you."

The Sailor & The Miracle Ship

The news spread like wildfire that Chief Edwards, a Reserve Chief Boatswain Mate on the base, was a former shipmate of the Admiral. When Edwards would go through the mess line, he couldn't eat all the food they piled on his plate. Sailors would come up to him and ask him about the Miracle Ship and the naval battle at Guadalcanal and how in the world did they make it back to the states with 120 feet of the New Orleans blown away? For the rest of the two week tour, Edwards was treated royally. After the news spread around of his connection with Admiral Charbonnet he met Commander Ben Wallace who had thrown his weight around and had given him a hard time when he first arrived.

Edwards met him and saluted him one day.

"Chief, let's have a little talk," Commander Wallace said.

"Yes, sir," Edward said, wondering what this was all about."

"I was hard on you when you first arrived. I want to apologize. I expected things of you beyond the scope of your training. I was wrong."

"Think no more about it," Edwards said. "I wish you the best for the rest of your tour in the navy."

For the rest of Edward's stay in New Orleans, "sugar wouldn't melt in Commander Wallace's mouth" in his treatment of Chief Edwards.

ೲ About The Author ೲ

Chief Edwards was retired with honors from the United States Naval Reserve in December of 1978. His was a long and distinguished Naval career, spanning thirty-six years — much of it in the heat of battle as a teenager in World War II and then thirty-two years of notable service in the Naval Reserve. We owe a great debt of gratitude to him and to all men like him who, through the history of our great country, have laid their lives on the line, many of them giving their lives, to preserve the precious freedoms that we, too often, take for granted.

Chief Benjamin Porter Edwards now lives alone in Nashville, Tennessee. His wife, Aliene, the love of his life, passed away in February, 1998. The Chief is still active in mind and body and wades into worthwhile projects with even greater enthusiasm and determination than ever.

Olan Bassham

The Sailor & The Miracle Ship

Olan Bassham, co-author of this book.

Epilogue

As many people do, I often think back on the past, and I always think of the years of my life spent in the Navy during World War II, and Reserve in peace time. In some ways it seems like a dream. I separate my Naval career into six periods of time:

1. Boot Camp, August and September, 1942-Company 42-460.
2. U.S.S. New Orleans, October 4, 1942-December 10, 1943.
3. U.S.S. Cape Esperance, April, 1944-January, 1945.
4. Naval Shore Facilities 3964, Philippine Islands, June, 1945-March, 1946.
5. Discharge, June 5, 1946.
6. U.S. Navy Reserve, June, 1946 - November, 1978.

I enlisted in the Navy on August 14, 1942. They sent me to the Naval Training Center at San Diego, California for my basic training. On September 1, 1942, when I turned 17, I was in the process of Boot Camp training. From there we headed straight to the Solomon Islands to fight the Japanese.

ಜ Epilogue ಜ

On that dreadful night of November 30, 1942, in the battle of Tassafornga off Savo Island, everything went wrong. We grossly underestimated the ability of the enemy and their Commander Rear Admiral Raizo Tanaka. Also, our gunfire left much to be desired. They sank one of our heavy cruisers and put three others out of service for almost a year. It is sad and difficult to admit that this battle was a stunning defeat inflicted on an otherwise alert cruiser force by a partially surprised and inferior destroyer force. Not only was Rear Admiral Tanaka good that night, he was superb. He made no mistakes. The one major accomplishment of our ill-fated Task Force 67 on that November night of 1942, was that we prevented the Japs from reinforcing their troops on Guadalcanal. Soon thereafter, they gave up in the Solomon Islands, because they were never able to take Henderson Air Field on Guadalcanal.

Now I think an individual report of what happened to each of our ships of Task Force 67 is in order. Since the Northhampton was the only heavy cruiser sunk, we will start here. She was commanded by the able Captain Williard A. Kitts. Task Force 67 was composed of 4 heavy cruisers, one light cruiser and six destroyers. This powerful Naval Unit was under the command of Rear Admiral Carelton H. Wright. The cruisers, in battle

❧ Epilogue ❧

formation were stationed 1,000 yards apart. The flagship Minneapolis was first followed by the New Orleans, Pensacola, Honolulu and the Northhampton in that order. Each cruiser was torpedoed in their order of battle formation, except the light cruiser Honolulu.

The Northhampton was never able to join her damaged friends in Tulagi. Captain Kitt's crew fought a losing battle, handicapped by fire and unable to make the 18 miles to Tulagi. At 0150, destroyers Fletcher and Drayton arrived and began to rescue the Northhampton sailors from the water. At 0240 Captain Kitts and the salvage crew hit the water. Twenty-four minutes later the proud lady's long career came to an end as she quietly slid under the surface, stern first, to her grave in 600 fathoms of water. By daylight stout determined swimmers had rescued 773 men. Fifty-eight of the original crew were lost.

At 2327 as the Flagship Minneapolis triggered her ninth Salvo, two powerful warheads ripped into her hull, releasing vast explosive energy. On the bridge, Captain Charles E. Rosendahl wondered if his ship could survive the two powerful hits. Then to his astonishment and gratification, her eight inch guns resumed firing.

The New Orleans, next astern of the flagship overtook her so fast that Captain Clifford H. Roper had to order hard right rudder. The ramming of the ship was

ॐ Epilogue ॐ

avoided but it placed the ship in the direct path of an approaching enemy torpedo. It hit on the port side between Turret one and two. It was a triple blast of devastating force. We had the explosion of the torpedo, two magazines and the aviation gas. It blew our bow completely off. That's 120 feet of the ship. When the help of God and the outstanding work of our damage control parties, we were able to keep the "No Boat" afloat. While the ship was in a turn, the officer in turret three reported that he was ready to continue the fight.

Captain Frank L. Lowe, in command of the U.S.S. Pensacola, was in the anti-aircraft control station when a 21 inch surface torpedo launched from a Jap destroyer, hit her directly below the main mast on the port side. The hit flooded the after engine room, put three gun Turrets out of order, knocked out gyros and communications, ruptured oil tanks and made an oil soaked torch of the mast where trapped sailors were roasted to death.

The light cruiser U.S.S. Honolulu, was commanded by Captain Robert W. Hayler. This was the only cruiser spared the deadly accuracy of Rear Admiral Raizo Tanaka and his torpedo henchman. Since Captain Hayler was able to avoid damage to his ship, he was able to scout the area for the enemy. Shortly before daybreak the Honolulu found and sank an enemy destroyer.

ॐ Epilogue ॐ

A light cruiser carries 6 inch guns while a heavy cruiser carrier carries 8 inch guns.

The engineering plant of the New Orleans was in tact, power and lighting normal and fires under control. Captain Roper stayed on the bridge where he had a clear view ahead. Commander Riggs, the Executive Officer, remained aft to control steering and engines. She was able to turn up five knots, so the course was set for Tulagi Harbor. The destroyer Maury joined her at 0235 and they arrived at 0610 on December, 1. To avoid detection, the crew covered our ship from stem to stern with camouflage nets and tree branches. We tied up to trees in order to further avoid being seen.

Tulagi was one of the worst places I have ever seen. There was not a breath of fresh air to be had. But there were plenty of flies, mosquitoes, malaria and dysentery. Living under these conditions was bad enough, but we had to work under them. Tulagi was a base for repair of motor torpedo boats. Encouragement was about all the natives and repairmen could give us, and believe me we needed plenty of that. The New Orleans CA 32 later came to be known as the "Miracle Ship", the ship that refused to sink, the ship that saved herself. We read in the Bible about the many miracles Jesus did. I saw and lived one at the tender age of seventeen on the most damaged ship not to sink.

ꕤ Epilogue ꕤ

Our country has had some great Presidents like Washington, Lincoln, Jefferson, Jackson, Polk, Teddy Roosevelt, Wilson, Franklin D. Roosevelt, Truman. There were all great Commander-In-Chiefs but of all the Presidents, Generals, Admirals, Colonels and Captains, the greatest Commander-In-Chief is and always will be Jesus Christ. The many terrible wars that our wonderful country has had to fight, our Lord and Savior Jesus Christ has always seen fit to spare the good old USA The important thing is not so much for Him to be on our side, but rather for us to be on His side. Let us give thanks and pray that America will so respect Him and His will that God will always bless America.

In Jesus' Name,

Written by:

B. P. Edwards, Jr. (Pete) BMC, retired
1000 Mitchell Road
Nashville, Tennessee 37206

❧ Speech ❧

A speech by B. P. Edwards at Nashville Naval Reserve classified outstanding:

On October 13, 1775 the 2nd Continental Congress authorized the fitting out of 2 vessels. This was the small beginning of a surface fleet that would grow into a sea power second to none.

During the Revolutionary War, and into the nineteenth century warships were grouped into three major classes, namely: Sloops-of-war, 10 to 20 guns, Frigates, or cruisers of their day, 28 to 44 guns, and Ships-of-the Line, which were the Battle Ships of the sailing days. These ships were equipped with 64 to over 100 guns of various sizes.

Famous ships, and outstanding Navy Heroes always have a tendency to go together. The Alfred had the distinction of being the U.S. Navy's first Flagship and is said to be the first U.S. Ship on which the "Flag of Freedom" was hoisted by John Paul Jones. He was called, "The Father of the American Navy." Captain John Paul Jones was born in Scotland on July 6, 1747. He was commissioned as a lieutenant in the Continental Navy on December 7, 1775. During his Naval career he was in command of the Providence, Ranger, Bon Lomme Richard,

ᔍ Speech ᔍ

and The America. His reply to the British when they demanded him to surrender, was "I have not yet begun to fight," and this has become a famous Navy Slogan. Captain John Paul Jones wasn't elected to the Hall of Fame until 1925.

The war with Tripoli, and the War of 1812 saw bigger ships coming into the U.S. Navy. The Independence was our first ship of the line. The 74 gun North Carolina, authorized in 1816, was a true ancestor to the battleship and had an awesome punch.

Stephen Decatur was one of the most daring officers in the United States Navy in its early years. He is best remembered for his toast: "Our Country, in her relations with foreign nations may she always be right, but our country, right or wrong." Commodore Stephen Decatur enjoyed great popularity with his men and the public. He is one of the group of men that established the naval traditions of the United States. During the war with Tripoli, on the night of February 16, 1804, he led a picked band into the harbor and set fire to the Frigate Philadelphia; once commanded by his father, which the Tripoli pirates had captured. Not a man was killed and only one was wounded. The English Admiral Horatio Nelson, the greatest British Navy hero of all time, called this exploit, "The most bold and daring act of the age."

ఱ Speech ఱ

Because of it, Decatur won a sword from Congress and Captaincy when he was only 25. In 1813 he became a Commodore, and shortly thereafter, sailed against Algiers, Tunis, and Tripoli, when he forced the rulers to release U.S. ships and prisoners and stop molesting U.S. vessels.

Commodore Oliver Hazard Perry won an outstanding victory over the British Fleet in the War with England on September 10, 1813 at the Battle of Lake Erie. Perry then sent to General William henry Harrisor, the military commander in the West, the famous message: "We have met the enemy and they are outs." As a reward, Perry was promoted to the rank of Captain and received a gold medal and a vote of thanks, and $7,500 from Congress. He was also awarded $5,000 in prize money.

Commodore Matthew Cailbraith Perry, was the brother of Commodore Oliver H. Perry. He opened Japanese parts to world trade. He sailed the first U. S. Navy ships into Tokyo Bay on July 18, 1853. Perry greatly impressed Japan with a show of force and dignity. He arrived in Tokyo Bay with his decks cleared for action, and letters from President Millard Fillmore. He refused to deal with anyone except the highest officials. Perry's boldness succeeded. The opening of Japan ranks as one of history's most significant diplomatic achievements.

❧ Speech ❧

In The Mexican War from 1846 to 1848 Commodore Matthew Perry was in command of the Mississippi, and served as commander in chief of the squadron off the east coast of Mexico. His squadron was the largest under the U.S. Flag, at that time, and worked with Army forces led by General Winfield Scott in the siege and capture of Veracruz.

David Glasgaw Farraget was made a full Admiral in 1866 when the rank was created for him. He won fame during the Civil War at the Battle of Mobile Bay with his statement, "Damn the torpedoes. Full steam ahead." Admiral Farraget took command of the important Western Gulf Blockading Squadron and cooperated brilliantly with General B. F. Butler, and General E.R.S. Canby in operations against New Orleans and the forts at Mobile Bay. He won the nickname of "Old Salamander."

The factor that contributed greatly to the Spanish-American War of 1898 was the sinking of the armored cruiser Maine in Havana Harbor. She had been sent there because of the long, continued unrest in Spanish Cuba, with resultant loss of life and property to Americans, a condition of which Spain seemed unable to correct.

Admiral George Dewey was in Hong Kong in command of the Asiatic Squadron when war broke out. He received orders on April 26 to go to the Philippine

❧ Speech ❧

Islands and capture or destroy the Spanish Fleet. Late on April 30, Admiral Dewey's six ships, led by the U.S.S. Olympia approached Manila Bay. During the early morning hours on May 1, 1898, Admiral George Dewey, gave the captain of the Flagship Olympia the famous command: "You may fire when you are ready Gidlsy", and attacked the Spanish Fleet of 10 cruisers and gunboats. By noon, Admiral Dewey's force of 6 ships had destroyed the Spanish fleet without the loss of a single American life. This victory made the United States an important power in the Pacific Ocean, and inspired the confidence of the American people in the United States Navy. When Admiral Dewey returned to New York City in 1899, he received a great welcome. The people of the country donated funds to buy a home for him in Washington, DC The congress presented Admiral George Dewey with a sword and all his men were awarded medals. By a special act of the United States Congress he was made Admiral of the Navy. He is the only American even to become Admiral of the Navy.

Admiral Dewey was born on December 26, 1837, in Montpelier, Vermont. His first war time service came in the Civil War, in the year 1861. As a Lieutenant, he became the executive officer of the U.S.S. Mississippi in David Farrguts fleet. Later, he served on Farrguts Flag

❧ Speech ❧

ship. He became president of the newly created Gernal Board of the Navy Department in 1900. He served as an honored adviser on all naval matters until his death in 1917.

On April 6, 1917 Congress declared war on Germany. The direct cause for this declaration, bringing us formally into World War I was German's bold and deliberate act of unrestricted war. The contribution made by the United States Navy toward victory in World War I was logistic and defensive. This included furnishing supplies, transporting troops, and in providing convoy escorts and patrols which not so much destroyed submarines as kept them impotent. Yet this contribution was not only essential, it was made at a time when neither the British nor French could have made it for themselves. Thus on the part f the American Navy it was an unspectacular war. From the viewpoint of the Navy, it was a war of statistic, in which the effort was counted in terms of ships not sunk, and of good arms and troops delivered. In spite of these facts, the United States Navy, like all other wars is not without its men that gave of their skill and talent, far beyond the call of duty. Admiral William Sawden Sims advanced to Permanent rank of Rear Admiral when the war began. He shortly became the ranking Admiral of our European Fleet. He became a

❧ Speech ❧

Vice-Admiral and then Admiral in 1918. He won a Pulitzer prize in 1921 for *The Victory at Sea*, which he wrote with Burton Hendrick. The report of the Secretary of the Navy in 1919 stated: "His brilliant service abroad won world wide admiration and he demonstrated that he is worthy of the greatest honors congress can confer upon him." Admiral Sims became inspector of target practice for the Asiatic Squadron, and suggested a new system for target practice which greatly improved American Naval gunnery.

Of Admiral W. S. Benson, the Secretary of the Navy reported in 1918: "The distinguished Chief of Naval Operations honored at home and abroad for his wisdom, statesmanship, and for his ability in his profession has with his staff of experienced officers, rendered distinguished and important service.

On the morning of December 7, 1941, Vice-Admiral Chuichi Nagumo of the Imperial Japanese Navy had successfully led a 33 ship stricking force that steamed under the cover of darkness within 200 miles north of the Island of Oahu, Hawaii. His six carriers launched 360 torpedo and dive bombers. At about 0755 the devastating attack began on the 94 ships anchored in Pearl Harbor, Hawaii. The prime target was the 8 battleships, the

❧ Speech ❧

backbone of our Pacific Fleet. The Japanese came in five waves of dive bombers and torpedo plans from 6 carriers, and within an hour all 8 battleships of the Pacific Fleet were severely damaged, 2 of them permanently, one with her magazines blown up and the second capsized. All the others but one had their keels on the bottom and it would be a year before more than 3 of them would be repaired. There were 2,403 dead and 1,178 wounded, more than the United States Navy had lost in the Spanish War and World War I combined. Thus, the Unites States Navy had suffered its most humiliating defeat at the hands of a country smaller in area than the state of California. When President Franklin D. Roosevelt went before Congress on December 8, 1941, asking for a declaration of war on Japan, he referred to the sneak attack: "As a day of Infamy."

    Admiral Isoroku Yamamato commanded the combined Imperial Japanese Fleet at the time of the attack on Pearl Harbor in 1941. He was one of Japan's great Admirals, with a long distinguished career in war and peace. He received some of his education in the United States. He opposed the policies that led to war with America. But he sponsored the planning that led to the Pearl Harbor attack as Japan's only chance of victory. A few years prior to the attack, he was sharply ridiculed by military and civilian dignities when he suggested an attack

❧ Speech ❧

on the fleet in Pearl Harbor. He was told that because of the shallow depth of the harbor, that it would be impossible to use a conventional aerial torpedo. Pearl Harbor is 40 feet deep. He promptly countered: "A special shallow water aerial torpedo could be designed and perfected." Admiral Yamamato was killed in 1943 when his plane was shot down in the South Pacific.

One of the key factors for victory in the Pacific was due to the brilliant strategy and tactics employed by Fleet Admiral Chester William Nimitz. He served all but 10 days of the war as commander-in-chief of the Pacific Fleet. When he took command at Pearl Harbor, the morale of the Navy was at its lowest point in history. He directed both the Navy and the Marine Corps. His calm assurance of final victory did much to restore the Navy's faith in his own power and ability. His strategy was that he simply and absolutely refused to wear out the fleet in attacks before the American forces were fully ready, in spite of angry questions from congressman and newspapers. He led the Pacific fleet through victory after victory, until with overwhelming force it drove the Japanese back to their home land. Admiral Nimitz became Fleet Admiral in 1944, shortly after the 5 star rank had been introduced on December 14, 1944. He was born in Fredenicksburg, Texas on February 24, 1885. He signed for the United States at

Speech

the Japanese surrender ceremonies in Tokyo Bay. He succeeded Admiral Ernest King as Chief of Naval Operations after the war.

He was graduated from the U.S. Naval Academy in 1905. His first service was in China where he commanded the gunboat Panay that the Japanese sank in 1937. He later specialized in submarine duty, and during World War I he acted as Chief of staff to the commander of the Atlantic Submarine Fleet. He served as assistant chief of the Bureau of Navigation in 1935, and chief of the bureau, with the rank of Rear Admiral in 1939. When he left active duty in 1947, he became special assistant to the Secretary of the Navy. He headed the United Nations mediation commission in the dispute over Kashmire in 1949.

Nemitz was asked the question of what our chances of winning the war were; he answered; "The Lord gave us two ends to use, one to think with and one to sit with. The war depends on which we choose. Head we win, tails we lose."

Fleet Admiral William Frederick Halsey, Jr. Was one of the leading American Naval commanders in World War II. He led the first U.S. Naval attacks on the Gilbirts and Marshall islands in January 1942. In the fall of that year, his forces beat back a larger Japanese fleet and made possible American operations in the Solomon Islands. In

ও Speech ও

the last year of the war, Fleet Admiral Halsey's third Fleet drove the Japanese back to their homeland. Japan signed the surrender on Halsey's Flagship, the battleship Missouri. In the Battle for Leyte Gulf in the Philippines Islands, his Third Fleet, and Admiral Thomas Kineaid's Swerth Fleet smashed the Imperial Japanese Navy and virtually eliminated it from the war. General Douglas McAuthur called Halsey, "The greatest fighting Admiral" of World War II. His frequent "salty" remarks were widely quoted. Typical of Admiral Halsey was the order he gave a few minutes after the Japanese stopped fighting on August 15, 1945. He ordered all Japanese snooper on planes shot down "not in spirit of vengeance, but in a friendly fashion."

Admiral Halsey was born in Elizabeth, New Jersey in 1882 and was graduated from the United States Naval Academy in 1904. He retired with the rank of Fleet Admiral in 1947.

Admiral Marc Andrew Mitscher was one of the first U. S. Navy Officers to adapt aviation as a career. He commanded the famous Task Force 58, which played an important part in defeating Japan in World War II. In the 9 month period from January to October of 1944, Admiral Mistcher's forces sank or damaged 795 Japanese ships and destroyed 4,425 enemy planes. He received the

❧ Speech ❧

Distinguished Service Medal three times. He took command of the aircraft carrier Hornet in October, 1941, and on April 18, 1942, General James Dolittle's planes made the first air raid of the war on Japan after taking off from the decks of the Hornet. After World War II, Admiral Mitscher became Deputy Chief of Naval Operations for Air. He became a full Admiral on March 1, 1946, and took command of the Eighth Fleet in the Atlantic. He was born in Hillsboro, Wisconsin in 1887, and was graduated from the United States Naval Academy in 1910. Admiral Mitscher learned to fly in 1915, and was the 32nd Naval officer to receive his "wings." In 1934, he became Executive Officer of the aircraft Carrier Saratoga.

Admiral Anleigh Alhert Burke was one of the ablest naval officers of World War II. He first won recognition during 1943 and 1944 for his excellent handling of destroyers in the South Pacific. Here he acquired the nickname "31-Knot Burke." His destroyer Squadron 23, known as the "Little Beavers" covered the landings on Boanvill, and fought in 23 separate engagements against the Japanese. Later Admiral Burke served as Chief of Staff to the Commander, Fast Carrier Task Force 58. During the Korean War, he was deputy chief of staff to the commander of Naval forces in the far east. Later he became a member of the United Nations Truce Delegation.

❧ Speech ❧

He served as Chief of Naval Operations from 1955 to 1961. He retired from the U.S. Navy in 1961 at the age of 60.

Admiral Hymor George Rickover was born in 1900 in Warsaw, Poland, and came to this country with his parents when he was four years old. He pioneered the development of the U.S.S. Natilus, the first nucleon-powered submarine. Congress gave him a gold medal in 1959 for his achievements in developing nucleon power. In 1947 Admiral Richover became head of the Naval Reactors Branch of the U.S. Atomic Energy Commission. He also served as head of the Nucleon Power Division of the U.S. Navy. He was promoted to the rank of Vice-Admiral in 1959.

In concluding this tribute to outstanding American Naval Officers, I should hardly think it would be complete without a few comments on the American Admiral Alfred Thayer Mahan. He wrote many books on naval strategy and the influence of sea power on a nation's affairs. He became one of the world's great authorities on sea power. His books influenced the naval policies of many nations. His great work, *The Influence of Sea Power Upon History, 1660-1783*, which he wrote in 1890, influenced President Theodore Roosevelt in his naval building program.

ಌ Speech ಌ

Admiral Mahan's importance in history is due to his thorough study of sea power. Mahan's studies convinced him that a country's strength on the sea is of great importance to its prosperity and its position in the world.

Admiral Alfred Mahan was born in West Point, N.Y. in 1840. He studied at Columbia University and at the United States Naval Academy. He was graduated in 1859, and served in the South Atlantic and Gulf of Mexico Squadrons during the Civil War. Mahan served as president of the Naval War College at Newport, Rhode Island in 1886 and in 1892. He retired from the Navy in 1896 after 37 years of active service. But he returned to serve on the Naval Board during the Spanish American War.

He tried, through his books to convince Americans of the importance of a powerful U.S. Naval Force. His works include: *Gulfland Inland Waters*, published in 1883, *The Influence of Sea Power upon the French Revolution and Empire, 1793-1812*, published in 1892; *Lessons of the War With Spain (1899), Armaments and Arbitration (1912)*. He also wrote his autobiography, *From Sail to Steam (1907)* and biographies of Farragut (1894) and Nelson (1897).

His books will live forever as a shining example that the pen is truly greater than the sword.

The Sailor & The Miracle Ship

Chief Edwards and wife Aliene (1977)

The Sailor & The Miracle Ship

Chief Edwards and family *(left to right)*
Sylvia, Chief Edwards, wife Aliene, Nelda, Martha, Joanna
(wife Aliene passed away February 1998)

The Sailor & The Miracle Ship

Chief Edwards and wife Aliene on their 40th wedding anniversary with daughter Joanna.